ASK YOUR ANGELS . . .

- Is a loving, lasting relationship in my future?
- Where will I meet my soul mate?
- How will I know that this person is the one?
- Is my partner being faithful, honest, and sincere with me?
- Are we ready to have children?
- Will I have a healthy pregnancy?
- Will my child have special talents and abilities?
- Is there any danger I will be fired or laid off from my current job?
- I hate my job. Should I quit?
- Is my boss happy with my work?
- What are the chances of a promotion?
- Is this the time to start my own business?
- What can I do to improve my financial situation?
- Do I have any health conditions I don't know about?
- Are members of my family in good health?
- How can I reduce stress in my life?
- What is the goal I should be working toward?

D1010421

Avon Books are available at special quantity discounts for bulk purchases for sales promotions, premiums, fund raising or educational use. Special books, or book excerpts, can also be created to fit specific needs.

For details write or telephone the office of the Director of Special Markets, Avon Books, Dept. FP, 1350 Avenue of the Americas, New York, New York 10019, 1-800-238-0658.

HOW TO TALK WITH YOUR ANGELS

KIM · O'NEILL

AVON BOOKS NEW YORK

If you purchased this book without a cover, you should be aware that this book is stolen property. It was reported as "unsold and destroyed" to the publisher, and neither the author nor the publisher has received any payment for this "stripped book."

HOW TO TALK WITH YOUR ANGELS is an original publication of Avon Books. This work has never before appeared in book form.

AVON BOOKS
A division of
The Hearst Corporation
1350 Avenue of the Americas
New York, New York 10019

Copyright © 1995 by Kim O'Neill
Published by arrangement with the author
Library of Congress Catalog Card Number: 95-94304
ISBN: 0-380-78194-8

All rights reserved, which includes the right to reproduce this book or portions thereof in any form whatsoever except as provided by the U.S. Copyright Law. For information address Patricia Teal Literary Agency, 2036 Vista del Rosa, Fullerton, California 92631.

First Avon Books Printing: November 1995

AVON TRADEMARK REG. U.S. PAT. OFF. AND IN OTHER COUNTRIES, MARCA REGIS-TRADA, HECHO EN U.S.A.

Printed in the U.S.A.

RA   10   9   8   7   6   5   4

Acknowledgments

I remain eternally grateful to the Angels who tangibly introduced me to the process of communicating with Angelic beings. In particular, I offer humble thanks to my Angel, John Reid, who started me on my spiritual journey with steadfast loyalty and patience and who repeatedly overlooked my fear, hesitancy, and self-doubt as I began my life purpose of channeling for others.

I feel privileged and honored to speak for all the Angelic beings who have placed their trust in me to voice their profound, motivating, and sometimes humorous insights to the clients who visit my office for private sessions.

My clients are a daily inspiration to me as I witness their courageous struggle to overcome and resolve difficult issues and ultimately prevail to triumph personally, professionally, and spiritually. My heartfelt thanks to them for their enthusiastic and unwavering support for this book.

My friend and colleague Karon Glass provided invaluable assistance in bringing this project to fruition with her extensive knowledge of grammar, punctuation, and her unyielding attention to detail.

Tom Glass, a computer genius, came to my rescue

on several occasions and prevented me from slitting my throat when my unreliable computer malfunctioned. I am very beholden to him.

I am very fortunate as a writer to have the wonderful opportunity of being represented by agent Patricia Teal, who has had faith in my project from its conception.

I also thank Carrie Feron for her editing prowess and creative insight that helped to bring my work into much greater clarity.

Finally, my love and respect to my mother, who has always showered me with unconditional love, guidance, and encouragement and who has made me believe that anything is possible.

Contents

❧ PART ONE ❧
INTRODUCTION TO ANGELS

Chapter One:
How I Met My Angels
3

Chapter Two:
Our Angelic Companions
13

Chapter Three:
What You Can Expect from Channeling
26

❧ PART TWO ❧
GETTING STARTED

Chapter Four:
The Step-by-Step Technique
37

Chapter Five:
Building Communication Skills
68

Chapter Six:
Developing Self-Awareness
90

Chapter Seven:
Discovering Your Personal History
109

Chapter Eight:
Building a Beautiful Life
132

Chapter Nine:
You're Off and Running!
154

Chapter Ten:
Questions and Answers
186

A Last Word
215

PART ONE

Introduction

to

Angels

CHAPTER ONE

❦

How I Met My Angels

From my earliest childhood recollections I can vividly remember the presence of special, unseen companions who talked with me, played with me, guided me, comforted me, and protected me. As a child, I fully accepted and believed in the reality of their existence.

One day I became suddenly curious about why such special companions would choose to play with ordinary little me. My companions explained they were my guardian Angels who were sent from heaven to guide and watch over me.

Although I couldn't see them, I could always hear their voices whispering gently to me inside my head, and I began to develop a method of communication with them that allowed us to privately talk back and forth, as if we were communicating over a telepathic telephone.

Even as a small child, I would practice communicating with my Angels by thinking about a question, and moments later, they would reply with an answer that I could readily understand.

It was so effortless and so much fun to practice, I discovered it didn't take any time at all for me to fully develop this communication with my Angels, and soon we became the best of friends.

Once I became confident of receiving information from my Angels, they began to expand our communication by providing me with psychic messages in the form of dreams while I slept.

Before the age of ten, I was having clairvoyant dreams that foretold births, deaths, final scores of professional athletics, natural disasters, plane crashes, and violent crime including kidnappings, rapes, and murders.

It was fascinating and very frightening as a child to have such vivid and explicit nightmares. My dreams were filled with sound, color, smells, and clear images of people, places, and things involved with the day's current events. Sleep was very much like being hooked into a psychic CNN.

I would get out of bed each day, eager to read the morning newspaper and explore screaming headlines and feature stories that described the exact events I had dreamt about just the night before. My intuitive messages were proven time and time again to be so specific and accurate, I developed total trust and a sense of reverence for the information my Angels were providing me.

Although I was consistently receiving factual, detailed psychic information, I was too shy to share it with anyone. The unique relationship with my Angels began when I was so young and became so natural a process to me that, as a child, I believed everyone else was having the same experience and was receiving the same clairvoyant information as I was. It never occurred to me that the communication with my Angels was in any way remarkable.

They continued to speak to me until I reached the age of eleven. Then my Angelic messages quieted, except for an occasional clairvoyant dream.

Surprisingly, I didn't miss receiving the intuitive information. With no psychic distractions, I could suddenly begin to focus all my attention on the "normal" girlhood interests of books, clothes, music, school, and boys. I'm sorry to say I soon forgot all about the special communication I had developed with my Angels.

My spiritual awakening didn't resume for many years. I didn't hear from my Angels again until I was in my early thirties and my life was in total chaos.

Professionally, I was the co-owner of a small advertising agency in Houston that was always teetering on the brink of insolvency. Plunging oil prices were completely devastating the Texas economy.

I was an emotional wreck, drowning in the stress and pressure of the highly competitive advertising industry. I tried to balance the financial concerns of meeting payroll with the creative challenges of working for demanding clients who complained about every invoice presented to them.

The labor-intensive, fast-track nature of the agency business was also affecting my physical health. Ignoring my once-healthy eating habits, I gulped down fast food carry-out at my desk over brainstorming sessions with agency colleagues. My sleep was continually interrupted by perpetual tossing and turning as I worried frantically about meeting monthly business expenses.

Each day I knew I was killing myself with stress, but I had no earthly idea what else I could do if I left the advertising industry. I felt hopelessly trapped, like an animal caught in the glare of oncoming headlights.

My personal life was also in shambles. I had no real relationships outside of the agency, because the long hours made it impossible to carry on any kind of consistent friendships.

My partner in the advertising agency was my husband, and we fought constantly over differing business philosophies and broken commitments. As a married couple, we carried the stress from the business home with us each night, making it impossible after-hours to relax, recharge, or unwind.

Feeling like a total failure, it took all the strength I could muster to put one foot in front of the other to survive each day as best I could.

Suddenly and without warning, at the lowest point of my life, the intuitive messages began again from my Angels. But this time, instead of gently bubbling into my consciousness as the messages did when I was a child, the intuitive information exploded inside of me.

It had been such a long time since I had any communication from them, I had completely forgotten about the Angels from my childhood. This startling, newfound intuitiveness created an enormous amount of confusion and distraction for me, dramatically adding to the stress I was already feeling.

I was "picking up" psychic energy from everyone and anyone who came near me. The intuitive information from my Angels came into my head loud and clear, just as it had when I was a child.

The girl standing next to me in the frozen food section of the grocery store was getting a divorce because her husband was unfaithful. The man who worked at the dry cleaners needed an antibiotic because he had a nasty bacterial infection. The doorman who worked in my apartment building needed to call his sister in Florida because she was just about to get test results that confirmed she had cancer. My client who worked in management for a drug rehabilitation center was finally going to be appointed president of the organization. My secretary was going to meet her Mr. Wonderful and be married within the year. My pregnant hairdresser was going to have a little girl who would grow up to become a famous heart surgeon.

I was suddenly besieged with a myriad of psychic awareness, and I couldn't turn it off. I hated what was happening! I could no longer focus or concentrate singly on my own thoughts, feelings, or desires as I had in the past. So many of my own thoughts were being pushed aside, as if now meaningless and unimportant, to clear the decks to make room for the psychic information I was receiving for other people.

Once I received an intuitive message for someone, it was repeated over and over and louder and louder inside my head, like a psychic telegram I was compelled to deliver. But I remained a very reluctant messenger, totally resistant to passing along the psychic information I was receiving.

How could I be certain that the intuitive information I was receiving was accurate? How could I pass along a psychic message to someone without being completely sure that I had "picked up" the information correctly? I began to remember how intuitive I was as a little girl, and how accurate and specific my information had been. But this was an entirely different situation.

I had never passed information along to other people when I was a child. It was very safe and non-threatening to check my psychic information by quietly reading a newspaper. What if I passed information along to someone and I was dead wrong about it? What if I got my signals crossed and needlessly scared someone? Or what if I got someone's hopes up for something that wasn't ever going to happen?

I began to feel a weighty responsibility along with the intuitive messages my Angels were providing, which I didn't like and didn't welcome. The last thing I needed was more responsibility. It was one thing to receive a great deal of clairvoyant information and keep it to myself. But I was beginning to realize that the reason I was receiving intuitive information as an adult was to pass it along to the people for whom it was intended.

No matter how "loud" the information became, there was absolutely no way that I was going to make a complete idiot of myself by approaching a business colleague and exclaiming, "Susan, I realize that you are now in upper management with XYZ Oil Company, but I want you to know that next year, you will move to Seattle and start your own consulting business." Or "Joe, please forgive me, I know we just met at the chamber of commerce after-hours networking dinner, but did you realize that you're going to marry your new secretary?" Or even worse, approaching a complete stranger, and blurting, "Hello . . . you don't know me, but I'm so happy to tell you that the test results will come back negative . . ."

The whole idea of passing psychic information along to other people was preposterous. I was a serious businesswoman. I was an entrepreneur who had worked very hard for many years to establish a professional and ethical reputation in the extremely conservative Houston business community. I couldn't fathom why this was happening to me. I was such a normal person.

I didn't have to be a brain surgeon to realize that if I began to pass psychic information along to other people, it would ruin me professionally. All the years of hard work would be destroyed. I'd become a laughingstock, and rightfully so.

I couldn't shake the feeling of hideous embarrassment of being labeled a psychic. Weren't psychics incredibly flaky, eccentric people who wore cheap, clanging jewelry, voluminous robes, heavy makeup, spoke in metaphysical mumbo-jumbo, and generally worked out of run-down trailers with neon palms in the front window? What about the psychics exposed by the media as fraudulent, preying on an unsuspecting public by selling potions and other ridiculous paraphernalia? Did I want to be connected with an industry like that?

But my brain was consumed with psychic messages. For months, despite my stubborn refusal, these messages kept coming. I finally realized that the Angels weren't going to give in or leave me in peace until I agreed to pass along the channeled information they were providing for other people. In desperation I decided I had no other choice.

During a weak spontaneous moment, and with serious misgivings, I decided to take the plunge. After careful deliberation, I chose the doorman at my apartment building as the first recipient of psychic information, because the message was urgent and had to do with his sister's health.

That fateful evening as I returned home from work, the doorman greeted me with a friendly smile.

I was grateful that we were alone in the lobby. My heart was pounding like crazy, my palms were sweaty, and my mouth was as dry as cotton. I smiled weakly, and walked up to him. I stood with my arms rigidly fixed by my side, leaned very close to him, and whispered nervously,

"How are you tonight, Frank?" My voice was a squeak.

The doorman's brows furrowed in surprise.

"You feeling okay, Miss O'Neill?"

If I didn't do it then, I knew I'd never do it at all.

"Frank," I blurted urgently, "your sister in Florida? She needs you to call her right away. She just received some test results from a biopsy and she'll be a little depressed and hearing your voice will make her feel better . . ."

Frank's eyes bulged out of his head and he quickly stepped away from me, putting a more comfortable distance between us.

"How did you know I have a sister in Florida?" he demanded suspiciously.

I didn't know how to answer him. I was hesitant to tell him the information came from my guardian Angels.

"Just call her, Frank. Tonight. Okay?"

His eyes still bulging, and his face now drained of color, Frank remained silent and took another few steps away from me as if worried about some kind of contamination.

"Well . . . good night Frank."

Frank only nodded.

As I walked to the elevators, I swore I'd never pass information along to anyone ever again. I felt like an idiot! I had never felt so ridiculous. I scared the hell out of the poor man and now he'd avoid me like the plague. Then I realized that he'd probably tell everyone else in the building that I was a kook, and the other tenants would probably avoid me, too! I hadn't considered that!

And what if the information about his sister was wrong? Had I worried him needlessly? Also, I guessed from his reaction that he would never call his sister.

I went to bed early that night, but was unable to sleep. I felt utterly humiliated. How could I have been so impetuous? I sensed that my Angels were overjoyed that I had passed the psychic information along, and I knew they were going to encourage and support me to do more of the same with other people. But I couldn't shake the mental picture of the astonished expression on Frank's face.

How could I ever live it down? I decided my only course of action was to avoid Frank completely in the future. Optimistically, I believed if he didn't see me, he might forget about the whole incident.

I walked quickly through the lobby the following morning with my head down in embarrassment and partially hidden behind my briefcase.

I heard a familiar voice shout my name. I grimaced and reluctantly turned to see Frank, the evening doorman, uncharacteristically still in the building. He scurried up to me, his face red with excitement and his eyes bulging even more than they had the night before.

"Miss O'Neill! I've been waiting for you! You were right! You were right! Sara has cancer!"

"Sara?" I asked stupidly.

"My sister! In Florida! At first, I thought you were crazy . . . no offense . . . but something told me to go ahead and call her anyway! She just got her results back yesterday! It's cancer, but her doctors say it's contained and she'll recover just fine. You were right! I just couldn't believe it! I would have never called her except for you . . ."

I was flabbergasted. I breathed a huge sigh of relief that my information was correct. While Frank continued to tell me about his sister, I heard my Angels say, "See! We're providing information to you that other people really need. This is only the beginning."

CHAPTER TWO

Our Angelic Companions

I am well aware that many will say that no one can possibly speak with spirits and angels so long as he is living in the body; many say it is all fancy, others that I recount such things to win credence, while others will make other kinds of objection. But I am deterred by none of these: for I have seen, I have heard, I have felt.

—EMANUEL SWEDENBORG

Who Are Angels?

Angels are the true unsung heroes of the universe. They are the embodiment of selfless devotion, limitless patience, unconditional love, and resolute determination.

Although we may not always be aware of their presence, we have the great privilege of being wrapped in an invisible cocoon of Angelic support, encouragement, love, and protection throughout our lives.

All life exists on two basic planes. There is the *physical* plane, where we live with a physical body, and there is the *spiritual* plane, which many people refer to as heaven. We know we currently exist on the physical plane because we have a physical body. When our physical body expires, our soul travels to heaven where we live quite comfortably until we decide to return to the physical plane to begin another lifetime.

I am frequently asked in my Angel seminars that if in fact we travel to heaven, why would we ever decide to return to the physical plane?

The reason is that only on the physical plane do we have the opportunity to build greater wisdom, enlightenment, and maturity. That is why life can be such a struggle. Life on the physical plane is meant to be a series of hard learning experiences, one after the other.

How do we learn to cope with hardships? How do we suffer setback after setback and still maintain our ability to set goals and follow our dreams? How can some people endure physical or mental disabilities and yet remain positive and optimistic? How do people encounter trauma and tragedy, and still go on to make a difference in the world?

The reason we are able to endure such hardships on the physical plane and still have the opportunity to build a life full of accomplishment and achievement is due primarily to the existence of our guardian Angels.

While it is true that guardian Angels live on the spiritual plane, not all heavenly beings have the opportunity to become guardian Angels.

In order to meet Angelic requirements, souls must be of the highest level of spiritual enlightenment and wisdom, and have proven themselves trustworthy to work tirelessly and in the best interest of those whom they guide.

The prospective Angel must be formally sanctioned by God and the other Angels in the universe to be allowed to perform Angelic work with those of us here on the physical plane. No being is ever sanctioned by the Universe unless he is of the highest spiritual evolvement, which dispels the common misconception about the existence of low-level, evil, or mischievous Angels. We never have to be concerned about attracting a "low-level" Angel who could create chaos in our life, because only those beings who have the highest respect for our spiritual progress, emotional sensitivity, and personal dignity would ever be sanctioned to work as a guardian Angel.

Angels live in heaven, but spend most of their time and considerable energy visiting the physical plane working shoulder to shoulder with the person they are assigned to guide and direct. An Angel's entire existence is based upon his or her resolute determination to help us accomplish as much as possible spiritually, personally, and professionally.

We are all individually assigned at least two guardian Angels as companions who work beside us twenty-four hours a day, every day of our lives, to help steer us through the difficulties we encounter by providing insight, awareness, support, and encouragement.

Our Angels are assigned to us according to two different criteria. First, an Angel must have prior experience with the type of challenges or issues we are to face and must have a higher level of wisdom and enlightenment than we do.

Second, the Angel must have a personality that

will mesh with ours, or the relationship won't be productive or fruitful.

The unique qualifications an Angel brings to the relationship determines the capacity in which they will work with you. In other words, each Angel assigned to you will be available to help you in very specific, yet different areas of your life. The Angel that assists you with personal relationships would generally not help you with professional issues, or with your health or safety. We all have so many facets to our lives, that we normally require substantially more than two Angels working with us at any one time.

Angels remain with you only as long as they are an integral part of your spiritual evolvement, which means they may remain by your side over the course of many lifetimes, or find it necessary to depart after only several days. You require new Angels each time you begin a new chapter of your life or when you are facing a whole new set of challenges. The more rapidly you move forward to meet new challenges and resolve issues, the more accelerated the transition for the Angels who are working with you. I refer to this transition as a "changing of the guard."

Providing unfailing support and encouragement, your guardian Angels focus entirely on what is most advantageous for you, and you'll quickly discover they are the most constant and steadfast companions you've ever had.

In spite of the loving intentions of family and friends, their advice and counsel can be colored by their own unresolved personal issues.

For instance, imagine that your biggest dream in life is to move to Florence, Italy and write a book about art history. After securing a steady but menial job while enjoying an Italian holiday, you decide to pack your belongings and relocate. You have an intuitive awareness that you'll never have a better opportunity to accomplish your dream. Several weeks later, while having dinner with a friend, you excitedly discuss your plans to move. The idea is met with anxiety and consternation by your friend, who becomes visibly upset.

The friend expresses significant concern for your emotional and financial well-being and states very pointedly that she thinks you're absolutely crazy and immature to even consider such a move. Although you know your friend loves you and wants the very best for you, she is actually voicing her own unresolved issues involving fear of independence, empowerment, and risk taking.

However, if you were to ask your Angels about moving to Florence, they would respond with very positive feedback because your trip is vital to your spiritual evolvement, personal fulfillment, and professional satisfaction.

Unlike your loving, well-meaning family and friends, your Angels provide information that is not filtered or colored by their unresolved personal issues. Instead, Angels focus entirely on what is most productive for *you* in terms of helping you create the best possible quality of life.

In addition, your Angels are always available to you. They never go on vacation, and they'll never refuse to communicate with you because they're eating, sleeping, or watching television. And you'll never be subjected to an Angelic answering machine.

The greatest purpose your Angels have is to facilitate a fuller awareness of what *could* happen in your life, what *is* happening in your life, and *why* certain events or situations are taking place. Your Angels are consistently working to provide this information to you.

When I have a private session with a client in my office, I channel information for him or her directly from his or her guardian Angels. Quite often, an Angel will complain to me that the person she is to guide is ignoring her, is very blocked, or is skeptical of the whole intuitive process.

For this reason, there are a vast number of Angels who walk among us in physical form to more tangibly direct and assist the people for whom they work.

What does an Angel look like who has taken a physical form? Just like you and me. The boy who helps you with your groceries could be an Angel. So could the woman behind the dry cleaning counter. Or your guardian Angel could be the CPA who has just completed your taxes.

When Angels are given the opportunity to take physical form, they move directly to the place where most of their "guidees" have congregated. They relocate to an area on the physical plane where they are needed most. Their divine philosophy is based upon the fact that it is much easier to accept an Angel in human form than an Angel who is in spirit form.

All human beings have the inborn ability to directly communicate with their own individual guardian Angels. If you build an awareness of your Angelic companions and develop your skills in communicating with them, together you can dramatically increase your ability to swiftly recognize and grasp opportunities, more readily discover solutions to problems, and reach the highest possible levels of success, happiness, peace of mind, and fulfillment.

How Angels Talk to Us

Many people tell me that they believe in the existence of guardian Angels, but aren't convinced that they have exclusive Angels who are individually working with them. After all, they reason, wouldn't they be aware of the presence of an Angel? Wouldn't they know that their Angels were speaking with them? Wouldn't they have some kind of evidence of Angelic communication?

We all receive proof of the existence of our guardian Angels every day of our lives. How is this possible? How can we be participants in such ongoing communication with our Angels, and yet remain oblivious to the relationship?

Our Angels begin their relationship with us while we are still tiny babies. Their presence remains such a constant in our lives and their communication with us is so subtle, that we naturally confuse the communication we receive from them with our own intuition or gut instincts.

When you develop an understanding of how your guardian Angels communicate, you'll start to develop a fuller sensitivity to their presence, you'll begin to recognize just how much information they provide to you, and you'll build the ability to access much more information from them than ever before.

Your Angels speak to you in three basic methods of communication:

1. The most common method of Angelic communication is *knowingness*. This basic form of conversation begins when you are a baby and continues through the rest of your life. Knowingness is the

most difficult form of Angelic communication to perceive because it is delivered subtly to you through your thought processes. You naturally believe the information is coming directly from your head, rather than from your Angels. The quickest and easiest way to recognize this form of Angelic communication is to become more aware of intuitive "feelings" and to listen to that little voice inside your head.

For example, imagine you are driving home from work and it begins to storm. A little voice inside your head tells you not to take your normal route because the street will be unpassable. You decide to follow your "instincts" and use an alternate road to reach your destination safely. You finally get home and turn on the television to watch news reports of the weather conditions. The street you normally travel is reported to be severely flooding and many motorists have been stranded because of high waters. You sigh with relief because you listened to your "inner voice." But it was more than your inner voice: your Angels were providing the information to you.

2. Although Angels communicate with *everyone* through the process of knowingness, it is also common for your Angels to speak to you with their own voices, just as a friend would talk to you over the telephone. Many people in my channeling seminars tell me that they first experienced this form of Angelic communication while they slept, usually between the hours of three and four in the morning. Angels often chose that time to make contact because you are a captive audience and are not distracted by outside stimuli as you

are during waking hours. It is much more difficult to ignore their messages in the quiet, wee hours of the morning.

If they've encountered stumbling blocks in their attempts to reach you through knowingness, Angels will often make their voices sound human in an attempt to get your attention. They will softly call your name to lull you out of a sound sleep. After you are awake, they will once again attempt to provide information to you through the process of knowingness.

A perfect example of someone hearing the voice of an Angel is depicted all through the movie *Field of Dreams*, as Kevin Costner received the Angelic information, "If you build it, they will come," directing him to build his backyard ballpark.

For example, imagine you are gently awakened in the middle of the night by a voice softly calling your name. You sit up in bed, trying to figure out where the voice came from. The cat is soundly sleeping at the foot of the bed and your significant other is contentedly snoring beside you. The voice couldn't have come from either of them, but you know you heard it. You look at the bedside clock and it reads 3:30 a.m. The voice does not speak again, but you are wide awake and find it impossible to return to sleep. Suddenly, you start picking up intuitive "feelings" about a certain situation at work that has caused you great stress and pressure. Angelic information about your boss and several co-workers continues to flood into your head for several minutes, until you have reached a new awareness and a greater understanding of the troubled situation. You quickly return to a restful sleep, comforted by a security you have not felt for a long time.

3. Angels provide intuitive information to you through *imagery* usually received in dreams. Visual imagery provides you a clear and vivid picture of people, places, and things. The visions may represent events that are currently taking place or events that will take place in the future. They may be messages that warn you about something or someone, or even past lifetime memories that are flooding to the surface of your consciousness.

This kind of communication can also be experienced during waking hours. In the movie *The Eyes of Laura Mars,* the photographer portrayed by Faye Dunaway receives vivid intuitive images of a string of murders. This is a perfect, though fictional, example of someone receiving visual imagery when she is awake.

Learning to Interpret Angelic Messages

Now that you are aware of the three ways your Angels communicate, you are ready to learn about the two distinct types of intuitive information they will provide to you during the communication process.

As you learn to differentiate between the two different types of Angelic messages, you'll also be learning to capably interpret the intuitive information they provide.

The first type of Angelic information is *literal* information. This is intuitive information you receive that is simple and easy to decipher.

For example, you might have a "feeling" about a promotion at work, an impending earthquake, meeting a wonderful man, or an illness in the family. The information is very clear and easy to understand and it is presented to you in a very straightforward manner.

After you have this "feeling," the event or situation you intuitively sensed actually occurs just the way you felt it would.

Symbolic information is another form of intuitive message passed on to you, often at night in the form of dreams. Symbolic information can initially seem vague or mystifying, and to understand the Angelic message, you have to interpret it correctly. Learning to interpret your dreams is a fascinating part of building your Angelic communication. It's very much like being a psychic detective. With just a little practice, you'll be interpreting symbolic information effortlessly and with enthusiasm.

For example, you might dream all night long about a white horse running through a meadow. Initially, this makes no sense to you. You don't own a horse, and you certainly aren't spending any time in a meadow. The literal message makes no immediate sense, so the dream must be symbolic in nature. To understand the message your Angels are trying to convey, you have to interpret it.

For example, you might interpret the dream as follows: The white horse represents and is symbolic of freedom, which you might feel you are sorely lacking at work or some other area of your life. The horse is white because that color represents your pure intentions, not only in the desire for more freedom, but also in the urge to move forward into your true life's work. The meadow could represent the peace and tranquility that you might feel if you actually broke free from your current employment and moved in your own direction, perhaps even setting up shop on your own.

As a side note, I don't believe in the validity of books or manuals that explain all the symbolism in dreams. People receive the symbolism that is right and meaningful for them at the time of their dream.

If I dream about a white horse and you dream about a white horse, it's silly and counterproductive to assume that the image of the white horse means exactly the same thing to both of us.

Each one of us is as individual as a snowflake. At this moment, we probably have very different issues. We have different people in our lives, and most likely we have a different life's work to accomplish. How could we possibly both dream about a white horse and have it mean the same thing?

Another interesting note: each time we dream about the white horse, it may not represent the same concept. Our Angels may be trying to pass along totally different information and may use the image of the white horse to symbolize something else entirely.

So how do you differentiate between literal and symbolic information? It's actually very simple.

After you receive your intuitive message in the form of a psychic "feeling," or hear an Angelic voice speaking to you, or see an image that is clear and easy to understand, you can rest assured that you have received literal information.

However, if after you have received your intuitive message in a dream, for example, and you're confused because the message doesn't appear to make immediate sense to you, you have received symbolic information. When you decide the nature of your Angelic message is symbolic, you need to correctly interpret it to learn exactly what your Angels are trying to convey to you.

Why do your Angels convey both literal and symbolic information to you? Why don't they just make it easier by providing only *literal* information that you don't have to work to interpret?

Because by learning to recognize symbolic information, and then building the skills to correctly interpret it, you are significantly developing your intuitive ability to communicate with your Angels. And by developing this heightened communication, you are ensuring that no Angelic information will slip through the cracks and be lost to you.

The intuitive interpretive process is similar to the way a detective works to uncover difficult or hidden clues. Instead of solving a crime, you'll be discovering exactly what your Angels are trying to tell you to help make your life more enriching, satisfying, and enjoyable.

Now that you are aware of how your Angels speak to you and the two types of information they provide, you are ready to learn how to actually speak directly with them through the process of channeling, as outlined in Chapters Three and Four.

CHAPTER THREE

What You Can Expect from Channeling

What Is Channeling?

Channeling is the ability to fluently communicate with any being who exists on the spiritual plane, which can also be referred to as heaven.

Most importantly, channeling allows you to communicate with heavenly beings like Angels, as well as deceased friends and family members who are now in heaven.

By now you may be enthusiastic about receiving Angelic information, and you are already familiar with the little voice inside your head (or psychic "feelings") that directs you in your decision making. But at times you probably feel frustrated because you'd like to access more specific intuitive information.

Up to this point, you most likely have to patiently wait for intuitive information to come to you from your guardian Angels. Unfortunately, when it does, you might miss it altogether because of outside distractions, or you might receive it in bits and pieces, like a radio station that fades in and out.

You may also be uncertain about exactly what your Angels are trying to tell you, and whether you've interpreted their Angelic information correctly. This one-way communication process can become very frustrating.

Developing your channeling ability will allow you to make direct contact with your guardian Angels at any time of the day or night. You can receive whatever information you desire clearly and in its entirety, without having to wait for them to come to you. Now you'll be establishing an astounding *two-way* communication that will provide you with more accurate and specific Angelic information than you ever dreamed possible.

The process of channeling will also allow you to fully and actively continue a relationship with a loved one who has moved to the spiritual plane.

Many of my clients who have suffered a loss ask if it is possible to communicate with a loved one who has "passed on." Their tremendous sense of loss has fueled a belief in an afterlife where a loved one peacefully exists and can still be contacted.

When someone dies, many people desperately want to know the whereabouts of the deceased and to be reassured that the loved one is "okay," but they don't want anyone to cruelly delude or patronize them.

Whether we exist here on the physical plane with a physical body or live in heaven without one, we are all a part of the same universe. There are no boundaries between the physical plane and the spiritual plane except those that we create and maintain in our own minds.

Because we are all a part of the same universe, and there is no separation between the physical and spiritual planes, we have an inborn ability to freely communicate back and forth as if connected by telephone lines.

Some people feel that their deceased loved ones frequently visit them, and can sense their presences because the familiarity of their energy is easy to recognize. You know your Uncle Herbert, so whether he exists on the physical plane with a physical body or has passed to the other plane and exists as a spirit, you'll know it's Uncle Herbert who visited you last night, and no one could convince you otherwise.

Sometimes our deceased loved ones visit us while we are awake, and on other occasions they choose to visit us in our dreams. The relationship we have with them can continue if we work to maintain and participate in direct communication with them. Channeling can help us to be active participants in relationships with those in heaven.

Many of us have had experience with deceased loved ones making contact by speaking to us, touching us, or even physically moving objects in our homes. After you recover from the initial surprise of "seeing" Uncle Herbert, it can be remarkably comforting and reassuring to know that he is okay, and that he wants to maintain a relationship with you.

A visitation from a loved one in spirit form is a common occurrence, so the event doesn't need to shock or frighten us. Most people who experience his communication become fascinated by the phenomenon and openly discuss their experiences with true faith and conviction.

Quite often, deceased loved ones visit us to pass along information that will protect us or bring us happiness and health. It is definitely in our best interests to be open and welcoming of these visits.

I'm convinced that everyone receives some form of contact from a deceased loved one, but can remain unaware of the communication if they are closed, blocked, or disbelieving.

While it is certainly possible for Uncle Herbert to contact you here on the physical plane, it is just as possible for you to initiate contact with him on the spiritual plane. I often do this in my office for clients who are afraid or skeptical.

The process of channeling is an easy way for us to have direct, two-way communication with those on the spiritual plane. As you build the ability to converse with your guardian Angels, you will also be developing communication skills that will allow you to make contact with your beloved Uncle Herbert. You no longer have to wait for *him* to come to *you*.

Along with communicating with your guardian Angels and deceased loved ones, your ability to channel will allow you to make contact with other beings from the spiritual plane who will make themselves available to speak with you.

I am frequently asked what Angels and other spiritual beings look like to me when I channel with them, since they no longer possess physical bodies. Often they present themselves to me looking exactly the way they did in their last physical lifetime. It's interesting and challenging for me to describe a spiritual being's appearance to my clients, including period hairstyles, modes of dress, styles of jewelry, material items they might be holding, and even fragrances they wore. Marilyn Monroe is an Angel for one of my male clients, and every time he has a private session with me, her fragrance of choice, Chanel No. 5, permeates my entire office.

Will you be able to make contact with any individual of your choosing on the other plane? No, not always. If the spiritual being has already returned to the physical plane and now exists here with a physical body as we do, it would obviously be impossible to channel with them. If the spiritual being is not acting as one of your guardian Angels and is not a deceased loved one, they may be busy with other important tasks and might ask you to make contact at a later time. Generally speaking, I have had great success in communicating with spiritual beings and have discovered that most often, they will make themselves available to speak with those of us here on the physical plane.

Why Should You Learn to Channel?

Learning to channel will open intuitive doors for you, free you from self-imposed limitations, and widen your spiritual horizons to an extent you never dreamed possible.

As you weigh the logical and pragmatic advantages of developing this ability to communicate with your Angels, you'll discover unexpected benefits from the information they provide to you that will have a great impact on your day-to-day existence.

Your Angels Can Protect You Against Physical Violence

Protecting you and your loved ones against physical violence is one of the most important daily functions of your guardian Angels.

Whether you live in the middle of a big congested city, a rural area, or a small town, there is a chance today that you will be the victim of a violent crime. It is your personal responsibility to learn to protect yourself and your loved ones.

Many people are "arming" themselves in anticipation of violent confrontations inside and outside their homes. Sales of shrieking alarms, mace, tear gas, firearms, knives, and other sharp objects are on the rise, but often the buyer discovers that these methods of protection do little to ensure their safety and may be used against them by a criminal.

A true safety device is one that serves to prevent or defuse the possibility of a violent confrontation with a criminal *before it happens*. Doesn't it make more sense to use a safety device that would allow you to completely avoid a confrontation altogether through prevention, rather than vulnerably react to one when it occurs?

Through the process of channeling, your guardian Angels can provide you with up-to-the-minute intuitive information about possible dangers in your immediate environment. You do not even need to specially request this information. It will be provided to you as needed to protect you and your loved ones.

In my channeling seminars, when I state that we are always protected by our Angels, people always ask about the victims of violent crime. If we all have our own guardian Angels, they ask, and if the Angels really warn us about the dangers we might be facing, why do many of us fall prey to criminals?

There are always risks in life, and some tragedies and accidents cannot be averted because in certain circumstances they are planned by the universe as a learning experience or a wake-up call. However, people sometimes become victims of violent crime because they aren't aware or simply don't listen to the warnings provided by their Angels.

For example, when I first began my channeling practice, I worked on many murder cases with the police, private investigators, and families of crime victims. In many cases, I psychically "saw" and "felt" the victim hearing a little voice inside their head warning them about potential danger, but he or she dismissed the intuitive warnings and suffered dire consequences. Unfortunately, women in particular need to be very aware of their personal safety.

How can you use your channeling ability to avoid being a victim of violent crime? It's very simple. Practice communicating with your Angels and *listen* to what they tell you.

Case in point: Several years ago, I was on a date with a gentleman who took me to the movies. We decided to visit the beautiful, new theater that had just opened in my neighborhood. After we stood in the concession line for our popcorn, we proceeded into the darkened theater. My date and I chose our seats and just as we began to talk, my Angels urgently warned, "Kim, get up and move immediately. Do not look around. Just get up and move."

The warning came so abruptly that it startled me. They repeated their warning, only this time their voices were yelling inside my head. I jumped to my feet and urged my confused date to move to another row of seats. We did and the Angelic voices softened, but continued to warn, "Don't look around. Stay in your seat, and don't look around."

Naturally, my curiosity got the best of me and I couldn't help but look around. The dimly lit theater was fairly empty, and I heard my Angels voice their warning again, but it was too late. Across the row of seats, exactly where we had just been sitting, was a young man of about twenty-five who was glaring at me with open hatred and hostility. His appearance was so sinister, dirty, and unkempt that I was surprised he had been admitted to the theater. When our eyes met, I shivered unpleasantly.

Then my Angels explained that the young man was the rapist who had been stalking women in the neighborhood. He especially liked to target potential victims when they were on dates. He would follow his victim and her escort to the woman's home and patiently wait for her date to leave. Then he would use force to enter the woman's home and sexually assault her.

My Angels told me not to be alarmed, and that they would protect me. I could feel the young man staring at me throughout the movie, but immediately after it was over, he left the theater quickly. I never saw him again.

I'm a fairly observant person, and it really scared me when I realized I sat right next to this man and never even noticed him. I know that my Angels helped prevent me from becoming his next victim. They protected me against the very real threat of physical violence by providing an unmistakable warning.

Since that time, because of my work with serious criminals and the families of crime victims, I have been in a number of potentially life-threatening situations.

My Angels have protected me with a wealth of preventive information that has allowed me to escape dangerous situations the way a gun or security device never could. By developing communication skills with your Angels, you'll be better able to receive and use their protection.

Your Angels Can Advise You About Your Health

Another very important function of your guardian Angels is to provide you with information about your physical health. Angelic information about your health is also usually *preventive*.

It is essential that we listen to what our Angels communicate to us about the state of our physical bodies.

Through our Angels, we have the opportunity to learn about potentially serious health conditions long before any symptoms arise, which could allow us to arrest or minimize the spread and the progression of a disease.

In some cases, prior knowledge of a likely health problem would immediately focus our attention on preventive measures years before the condition was expected to arise.

Your Angels can also assist you in understanding and working through difficult relationships, setting and achieving personal and professional goals, removing unnecessary stumbling blocks, and manifesting financial abundance.

PART TWO

Getting Started

CHAPTER FOUR

❧

The Step-by-Step Technique

N ow that you are familiar with Angels and have become aware of their divine purpose in working with you, you are finally ready to learn how to open communication with them.

This new learning process will be so easy and productive, you'll scarcely be able to believe that in such a short time, you're communicating with your own guardian Angels.

The simple nine-step process will be truly life-changing. Channeling with your Angels will open doors you never dreamed existed. No longer will you be limited to receiving the fragmented bits and pieces of intuitive information that you've been "picking up" before now. This process of developing a two-way communication with your Angels is much more like talking with a friend on the telephone. I refer to it as "hooking in."

You'll be able to call them and access Angelic information at any time of the day or night, without having to depend on anyone else to provide the information for you. I recommend you set aside fifteen minutes for your first attempt at channeling. More than likely, you won't need any more time than that to be successful at "hooking in."

A number of my clients have expressed amazement at how quickly they were directly communicating with their Angels. As human beings, it is our nature to make everything much more difficult and complicated than it has to be. Keep in mind that channeling is a completely natural process, much like breathing or sleeping, and as you've already learned in Chapter Two, you've been an experienced channeler since you were a tiny baby. The only difference in the techniques that follow is the way in which you will communicate with your Angels. The nine step technique is as follows.

Step One: Preparing to Talk with Your Angels

When you first attempt to channel, it is necessary to move to a quiet environment where you won't be disturbed or distracted by children, spouse, pets, radio, television, or the telephone. You'll need a quiet space to able to concentrate fully on the new form of communication you are learning. You'll also need a pen and a tablet of paper, or you may want to sit in front of your computer. After you are more experienced in talking with your Angels, however, you'll have the ability to speak with them in almost any environment.

Step Two: Developing Questions

When you initiate your two-way communication, speaking with your Angels will be easiest and most productive if you have prepared an agenda, or a list of questions. Write (or type) four or five questions that represent priorities to you. You may want to ask about family members, career, relationships, health, or any other topic, but make certain the questions are fairly specific. For example, the question, "How does my future look?" will be too vague, because your Angels won't know exactly what part of your future you are asking about. A better question would be, "How secure is my current job at ABC company?" or "Should I start my own business?"

Step Three: Initiating Contact

Reviewing your list of questions, choose the one you feel is most important, and then say aloud, "I wish to speak with my Angels. This is my first question . . ."

In the beginning, it is important to speak out loud to your Angels to establish in your mind that you are actually communicating with someone other than yourself; our minds tend to disbelieve anything that cannot be tangibly seen or felt.

Step Four: Asking for Information

After you have asked your first question, remain silent for a moment. You can usually expect to receive Angelic feedback in as little as fifteen to twenty seconds.

Step Five: Receiving an Angelic Response

Just as if you were speaking to a friend over the telephone, you will experience a timely response from your Angels that will be communicated to you in one of three ways, as discussed in Chapter Two:

1. *Knowingness,* which is the most common form of Angelic communication. Again, knowingness is the process of intuitive information suddenly "popping" into your head.

   After you have asked your first question, you will most likely receive an Angelic response that feels much the same as your gut instincts. It will be very gentle and subtle, but you won't have to strain to receive it. The answer to your first question may simply "pop" into your head.

2. Another way you might receive Angelic communication is by actually *hearing their voices* speaking directly to you. When you ask your first question, you may hear a soft voice provide the answer. Most often, people hear the voices of their Angels while they are sleeping, but this can also occur while you are awake.

3. Angels also choose to communicate to us through *visual imagery,* which is Angelic information seen as images in your mind's eye. While this often occurs when we dream, the same sensation of receiving intuitive information can occur while you are awake.

   For example: A mother is cleaning the kitchen after a family meal. While she completes the task, she asks her Angels about the safety and security of her children. She says aloud, "Is Jennifer, my youngest, safe from harm at this time?"

   Although the mother is looking directly at a sinkful of dirty dishes, she suddenly receives a flash of intuitive information in her mind's eye in response to her question. The mother psychically "witnesses" her youngest child chasing a ball into the street in front of the family home. A speeding car careens toward the child, and seconds later there is a horrific accident. In a sudden panic, the mother drops the dishcloth, runs outside to the spot where she "saw" the accident, and pulls the child from the street just as the speeding car is approaching.

In my Angel seminars, I've discovered that most people receive Angelic information through all three methods of communication. However, there may be times when you receive more information from your Angels by knowingness, or in hearing their voices, or through visual imagery. Your Angels will decide which method of communication best suits your changing needs as your ability to channel grows and as you continue building your spiritual foundation of wisdom, enlightenment, and maturity.

Step Six: Getting Confirmation

This is the exciting part! You've asked your specific question: "Should I start my own business?" You've waited several moments to receive your response. Suddenly, you experience a rush of information that feels like you are thinking, or talking to yourself:

"Yes, you should start your own business. This has been your dream for many years. And this is the perfect time! You will have the most happiness, sense of accomplishment, and financial security if you start a consulting business.

"Your college roommate has just moved into

town. Call her up; she would be an excellent business partner. She can provide some of the start-up capital. You need to move into your own business as soon as possible, not only because it is your dream, but also because you are becoming more and more miserable with your current job at ABC Company. And you will not receive the promotion and raise you expect in February . . .''

At this juncture, I guarantee that your brain will go into overdrive in an attempt to deny that this information is coming from an Angel. Until you become more experienced, and communicating with your Angels becomes as natural as breathing and sleeping, you will second-guess yourself like crazy. Expect it and be prepared. Ask yourself: ''How could I have known my college roommate had moved to my town? And I haven't started my own business for so long because I didn't know exactly what kind of business to start. I never thought about a consulting business! And how could I have predicted getting passed over for a raise and promotion that I fully expected?''

Ask yourself how you could have possibly become privy to those things on your own. You couldn't. It would be humanly impossible.

Even though you've assured yourself you could not have possibly picked up awareness of the answers without Angelic help, your brain is probably still in an immovable state of denial.

You have asked your Angel a specific question. You have received a response. Now, to confirm that you are indeed speaking to someone other than yourself, ask your Angel a second question: ''Are you really one of my Angels?''

Step Seven: The Hook-in

Your Angels will once again speak to you and confirm their presence. Their response may come in a rush of information that feels similar to thinking or talking to yourself:

"Yes, we are your Angels. We're so happy to be speaking to you in this way! We have so much information to give you . . ."

Now you are "hooked-in." From this point forward and for the rest of your life, you'll have the ability to access Angelic information whenever you want it. You have created a two-way communication with your Angels.

Note: If you don't feel you are receiving any information from your Angels and the silence is deafening, keep practicing and you'll be successful with the "hook in." The communication from your Angels will seem very soft-spoken and subtle at first. Don't expect them to hit you over the head with a frying pan. As you practice your communication skills with them, your Angels' voices will get louder and louder.

In all the years I've taught channeling, I've never had anyone complain that they had a continued problem learning to communicate with their Angels. Most people tell me that they accomplished the "hook in" on their first or second attempt. Remember, channeling is both an inherent gift and a learned skill.

A good part of building confidence in your ability to talk with your Angels will come from getting to know them. You will build relationships of mutual trust and respect, just as you would develop relationships with friends on this plane. And remember: your Angels are privy to behind-the-scenes awareness that you could have no way of knowing. With each communication you have with your Angels, the second-guessing will decrease until it completely disappears, and you'll have Angelic relationships that yield spectacular results.

Step Eight: Developing a Relationship with Your Angels

The information you'll receive from your Angels is limitless. Once you're hooked-in, ask your Angels to introduce themselves and describe in detail the exact purpose they have in working with you. The most productive relationship you can develop with your Angels will come from getting acquainted and building trust through communication.

Step Nine: Practice! Practice! Practice!

In order to build and develop the relationship with your Angels, it is absolutely necessary to practice your communication skills at least once a week for a fifteen-minute period. If you wish to spend more time talking with your Angels, that is even better.

After you have hooked-in, the more time you spend in practice, the more easily you will access information from your Angels. You will also discover how accurate and specific your Angelic information can be. Channeling will become a very natural process.

Another wonderful way to practice your Angelic communication skills is to suggest to spiritually open-minded family and friends that you'd be willing to ask their Angels for information for them. You'll be surprised at the wealth of knowledge and awareness you'll have the opportunity to provide to them from their Angels.

Asking the Right Questions

Now that you have learned to communicate with your Angels, the next important step is to learn to ask the right questions. Asking the right questions will help you access as much information as possible so that you can make intelligent and rewarding decisions.

Our Angels usually refrain from force-feeding information to us; their philosophy in working with us is one of patient respect. They wait until we have the awareness and maturity to think to ask certain questions before they volunteer the information.

In other words, if a six-year-old child approached you and asked where babies come from, you'd respond with the answer that would be appropriate and understandable for him at his age. If a thirteen-year-old approached you, the answer you'd give him would be totally different, but in keeping with his level of maturity. Our Angels work with us in the same way.

Case in point: You have fallen in love with a person who has never expressed any interest in getting married. The first question that occurs to you to ask your Angels probably is, "Will this person ever want to marry me?"

Additional, more important questions are: "Would I be happy and fulfilled if I did marry this person?" "Would our marriage last?" "Would this person be a good parent?"

Case in point: You are very unhappy where you're

working and have also been feeling insecure about your continued employment with your company. The first question that occurs to you to ask your Angels probably is, "Am I going to be laid off?"

That, of course, is a very important question to ask, but the answer to that question alone is not very enlightening. The more important questions are: "Where is my next career opportunity?" "What do I have to do to make it happen?" "How will I survive financially?"

The topics listed below represent a comprehensive source of prospective questions to ask your Angels. These questions can guard you against unnecessary challenges, stumbling blocks, and trauma. The answers will also make you much more aware of unknown or unexpected opportunities, assist you in developing marvelous relationships, and help you achieve financial security.

I had to reach a certain level of enlightenment before I even knew to ask questions like these. I have developed these questions through experience gained from hosting numerous seminars on communicating with Angels, as well as performing thousands of channeled sessions over a nine-year period.

Your Personal Life

A New Relationship

Congratulations! You've just met a very captivating person and sparks are flying. But before you eagerly leap into the unknown, possibly wasting your precious time or energy, you need to ask your Angels about the relationship's potential.

We all want to sidestep the possibility of falling in love with the wrong person—someone who could create unhappiness or chaos in our lives. Enduring difficult personal relationships can be extremely frustrating, annoying, distracting, and sometimes traumatic.

At the very beginning of a new relationship, your Angels can provide an awareness of why a person has come into your life, what purpose he serves, and how long he is meant to be with you.

When you understand the dynamics and purpose behind a new relationship, it is much easier to move forward comfortably. You will have complete awareness of what is possible in the relationship and what is not possible.

I strongly recommend you consider asking some or all of the following questions. Is this person:

- a Mr./Ms. Wonderful for me, or another hard learning experience?
- single?
- sure of his or her sexual preference?
- sexually compatible with me?
- struggling with unresolved issues?
- moving forward at a speed similar to my own?
- suffering from any addictions?
- suffering from a serious health condition?
- trustworthy, unselfish, willing to compromise, and open to new ideas?
- warm, cozy, affectionate, and loving?
- kind, compassionate, and nonjudgmental?
- controlling or manipulative?

- a good listener, as well as emotionally expressive and communicative?
- abusive physically or verbally?
- monogamous and loyal?
- funny and light-hearted?
- in a good relationship with his or her children, family, friends, and business colleagues?
- willing to develop a positive relationship with my children, family, siblings, friends, and business colleagues?
- from a family I can get along with (including children, ex-spouse, and parents)?
- willing to consider our relationship a top priority?
- able to honor commitments and promises to me?
- able to rise to the occasion and reach his or her full potential?
- willing to get married and have a lasting relationship?
- potentially a good partner?
- open to having children? Healthy pregnancies? How many? When? Girls? Boys?
- potentially a good parent?
- similar in values and lifestyle?
- settled in a career and able to meet financial goals?
- a giver or a taker?
- stable, mature, and consistent?
- intelligent and enlightened?
- my spiritual equal?

A Current Relationship

You've been with your significant other for some time and are curious about the future. Problems in the relationship might have led to gnawing dissatisfaction. Perhaps you are in a perfectly good relationship, but there are emotional or physical stumbling blocks that need to be resolved. You need information about what could happen if you stay in the relationship, and just as important, you need information about what you could encounter if you leave.

Unfortunately, some relationships, no matter how hard you try to make them otherwise, are meant to be difficult. I refer to them as *learning experiences*. Whether the relationship is personal or professional, the person has entered your life for a reason—to teach you about an issue on your spiritual agenda.

Before you get too annoyed about the whole process, understand that you provide the very same learning experience for the other person! It works both ways.

There is good news about relationships that are learning experiences. You are not impossibly stuck or trapped in them, although it may feel like it at the time. The key to resolving difficult relationships is learning about the issue and resolving it as quickly as possible. This frees you to leave the relationship and build a happier life.

You must ask your Angels *exactly* what issues you are working through with your current partner, because if you're not sure what they are, you could easily make the mistake of leaving the relationship prematurely.

That's why so many men and women end up repeating destructive patterns in relationships. They leave one person too soon and get involved with another who repeats the very same patterns.

The universe will provide difficult relationships for us until we finally learn from them and resolve our issues.

After your Angels have explained exactly what issues you are supposed to be working through, they will also communicate how you can work through them quickly.

Finally, your Angels will give you a progress report. They will be the first to congratulate you on the resolution of an issue, which means you are finished with the learning process and are ready to move on.

The answers to the following questions will clear up confusion about a current relationship, and will greatly help in your decision making. Is my partner:

- in love with me? Do I love him?
- a good choice for me at this time?
- a good parent?
- happy with our life? Am I happy? Why or why not?
- able to change? When? How?
- meant to be in my life for a long-term satisfying relationship or a short-term learning experience?
- working through his/her issues? Will he ever?
- honoring commitments to me? To the children?
- willing to get counseling or therapy if needed? Would we benefit from couples' counseling?
- making me his/her first priority?
- communicating his/her feelings to me?

- treating me with respect?
- able to keep promises?
- able to manage finances?
- faithful?
- honest and sincere with me?
- interested in continuing the relationship?

Also ask your Angels:

- If I stay, will the relationship get better? How will it get better? What are the chances of the relationship becoming verbally or physically abusive?
- Why were my partner and I first attracted to each other?
- What are supposed to be our learning experiences?
- Did we already accomplish everything we were meant to in the relationship?
- My partner has been abusive. Why can't I get this person out of my system?
- Should my partner and I separate or get a divorce?
- How will my partner react if I want to end the relationship?
- How will the children react if there is a divorce?
- If my partner reacts violently, how can I best protect myself? How can I best protect the children? How and when should I leave the marriage?
- Should I stay in the family home or should I move?
- Where should I go?

- Will I need a restraining or protective order?
- How can I find a good attorney?
- How long would a divorce take?
- Why am I so scared to move out of the relationship?
- Will my soon-to-be ex-spouse pay child support? Can I depend on its regular arrival?
- How will I support myself and the children?
- Should my partner continue a relationship with the children?
- Will my children want to continue a relationship with their father/mother?

A Future Relationship

You have no special person in your life right now and you wonder if perhaps you are just meant to be alone. Although you may not now have any immediate prospects for a serious relationship, it doesn't mean you'll never find that perfect partner!

Your Angels can provide specific information that will help make the lonely wait less frustrating.

In addition, your Angels can direct the building and maintaining of rewarding relationships while protectively steering you away from those that would prove unsatisfying or unproductive. Here are some questions you could ask your Angels:

- Do I have a Mr./Ms. Wonderful ever coming into my life? When?
- What can I do about loneliness in the meantime?

- Should I date a person who I know isn't the "right one"?

- Do I already know this special person?

- If not, how will we meet? Where?

- What does this person look like (eye color, hair color, height, age, etc.)?

- Will I find this person attractive immediately?

- Will this person find me attractive immediately?

- What does this person do for a living?

- Where does this person live?

- What is this person's marital background?

- Does this person have children? How many? What are their ages?

- Is this person enlightened, mature, and loving? Does he/she meet all my other criteria? In what ways?

- What will we do on our first date?

- When will we become a "couple"?

- Will we get married?

- Will we have children?

- Where will we live?

- Am I somehow slowing down the process of meeting this special person? Is there any work I have to do on my issues before I can meet this person?

- How will I know that this person is *the one?*

- Is this person prepared to secure the relationship?

- Will I like this person's family?

Pregnancy

When people ask me about relationships in a private channeled session, pregnancy is always one of the most popular topics. Depending on your particular age, lifestyle, partner, and a host of other variables, you might greatly desire a pregnancy at this time, or you might wish to prevent a pregnancy. This list of questions for your Angels will provide you with a wealth of behind-the-scenes intuitive information.

You Are Considering a Pregnancy

- Would I be a good parent?
- Would my partner be a good parent?
- How much would my partner share in the responsibilities?
- Do I want the lifelong bond of a child with my current partner?
- Would it be beneficial for me to wait to become pregnant? Why? And for how long?
- Is my partner ready for parenthood? Would he be enthusiastic about the pregnancy?
- How long will it take me to become pregnant?
- Do I have any physical problems that will prevent or prolong conception?
- If I do, what are the problems and what can I do, if anything, to correct them?
- Does my partner have any physical problems that will prevent or prolong conception?
- If he does, what are the problems and what can he do, if anything, to correct them?

- Will I have a healthy pregnancy?
- Are there any recommendations for diet, exercise, rest, reducing stress, etc., that would help make my pregnancy healthier or more comfortable?
- When will I give birth?
- What can I expect with this particular labor and delivery?
- Will I have any complications following the birth of my baby?
- Do I have the right doctor for me?
- If not, where will I find a better doctor (recommendation from a friend or from a doctor I respect)?
- What will be the gender of my child?
- Will this be a multiple birth?
- Will the child be healthy?
- If I can't conceive because of a health problem of mine or my partner's, what are the best alternatives? Artificial insemination? A surrogate mother? Adoption?
- If I choose adoption, which is the best agency for me?
- If I adopt, would I have any problems with the biological mother or father seeking future custody of the child?
- Do I need an attorney to help me with my search? If so, who would be the best attorney to help me?
- What will be my child's favorite foods, colors, toys, music?
- What are the special gifts and abilities my child will have?

- How can I best nurture and mentor my child to help him/her reach full potential?

You Are Not Considering a Pregnancy

- Have I effectively communicated my feelings about pregnancy to my partner?
- Am I pregnant at this time?
- Am I using the most effective method of birth control?
- Is there a more effective method of birth control I should consider to prevent pregnancy?
- Am I protecting myself completely against sexually transmitted diseases?
- What would be best for me if I accidentally became pregnant?

Your Professional Life

Where Are You Going?

When I give a private session in my office, clients ask one question more than any other. They worry that they are clueless about what direction their life should take. They have no sense of what their purpose is in life and no earthly idea when or how they will find it.

They have set no goals and as a result are helpless to achieve anything further. That's a very depressing and emotionally disabling thought to most people.

For example, if you truly believed that you were

never going to achieve more than you have right now, and that you'd never have the opportunity to create or build more, you'd probably feel like throwing yourself out of a very high window.

If you don't choose and set personal and professional goals for yourself and work toward them every day, your quality of life will remain exactly where it is right now.

Project ten years into the future. Do you want to be in the same place in your personal life? Do you want to be exactly where you are in your professional life?

You've probably answered, "Definitely not!" to both questions. If so, you need to finally make some decisions about what you do want to achieve next year, and the year after that, and the year after that.

You alone hold the key to creating whatever kind of life you desire. I can guarantee that your quality of life will not improve if you sit back and wait to become fulfilled and successful through the efforts of your significant other, parents, children, friends, or business colleagues. You can create the opportunity for improvement and move your life forward only through setting appropriate goals for yourself and sticking with them!

How can your Angels help you set and work toward your goals? Your Angels can give you all the information you need to know about your life's work and when you will have the opportunity to achieve it.

If your particular purpose in life is in a type of work that you don't have a lot of experience in, your Angels will explain how you can gain the experience and expertise to build success. They'll also tell you what you can expect in terms of satisfaction, accomplishment, and financial rewards.

Your Current Employment

- I was unexpectedly laid-off/fired from my last job and I don't believe the reason they gave me. What happened?

- Is there any danger of being fired or laid-off from my current job?

- What are the possibilities in my current job for greater income? Additional perks or benefits?

- Will I be offered a promotion? Can I move up within the company?

- If I move up within the company, will I like the new position?

- How long will I remain satisfied and fulfilled working at this company?

- Are my efforts recognized and appreciated?

- Is my boss happy with my performance? If not, what can be improved?

- Are my relationships with co-workers positive? If not, why am I experiencing friction or turmoil? What can I do about it?

- I hate my job! Should I leave the company?

- If I stay, will the working environment get any better? How? Why? How soon?

- How soon should I leave? To go where?

- What kind of job is best for me now? How will I get the new job? Employment service? Networking? Classified ads?

- Will I make more money at the new company?
- Will I really like my new job?
- Will I like and respect my new boss?
- Will I like my new co-workers?
- Will my new job be secure? How long would I work there?

Starting Your Own Business

- Is this the time to finally start my own business?
- Will I be happy with all the responsibility?
- Would I make a good boss?
- Should I sell a product or a service?
- How can I most effectively market my product/service? Mail order? Television? Radio? Newspapers? Networking?
- Should I take on a partner? Who?
- Where will I get my start-up capital?
- How should I legally set up my business? Should I incorporate?
- Would I be happier or more successful buying a franchise?
- Do I have a capable business attorney? If not, where can I find one?
- Do I have an ethical, knowledgeable CPA? If not, where can I find one?
- Where should I look for office space?
- How will I attract stable, competent employees?
- How will I keep stable, competent employees?

- How should I compensate my employees?

- How much money can I make the first year? The second year?

- If I start my own business, where will I be financially in five years? Ten years?

- My old business colleague/college roommate/ brother-in-law/neighbor/best friend/hairdresser, etc., asked me to go into business with him/her. Would we have a good relationship? Would he/she carry their end of the apple cart? Would this person honor commitments to me?

- Would we create financial security?

- How long would the business last? How long would the partnership last? How long would the friendship last?

You Own an Existing Business

- I already own my own business. How secure is it?

- Do I have a good relationship with my partner?

- Am I handling a fair level of responsibility?

- Is my partner handling a fair level of responsibility?

- Am I a good boss?

- Are my employees productive and happy?

- Do I have a capable business attorney? If not, where can I find one?

- Do I have an ethical, knowledgeable CPA? If not, where can I find one?

- Will the company's financial situation stay as it is? For how long?

- Am I completely aware of payables and receivables? Are all taxes being paid on time?

- What are the greatest opportunities for my company?

- Where is my industry headed in the future?

- Should I explore opportunities to merge with another company? Where and how would I find an appropriate match?

- Should I expand the products and/or services already offered by my company?

- If so, what type of products or services?

- Will the company be expanding? How soon?

- Will I need more employees? How many? Where will I get them?

- Will I have to move the company?

- What is the best location? Would this new locale offer room for expansion in the future?

Your Finances

Financially, your Angels can advise you on saving monies and investing resources to greatest advantage for the most substantial return.

Importantly, your Angels can also caution against a potentially disastrous financial situation that might deplete your savings or prove to be a financial burden for years to come.

- Will my current financial condition stay as it is? What can I do to improve it?

- Will I have money coming to me from an outside source? (Inheritance? The settlement of a lawsuit?)

- Will I encounter an event or a set of circumstances that will potentially deplete my financial resources or devastate me financially?

- What can I do, if anything, to prevent or sidestep these events?

- If I buy a house (or car, antiques, jewelry, stocks, private school for the children, plastic surgery, trip around the world, etc.) will it plunge me into bankruptcy or a miserable financial condition?

- Will I ever be secure enough financially to acquire a house (or car, antiques, etc.)? When? How?

- Do I have a capable attorney? If not, where can I find one?

- Am I filing an accurate annual income tax return to the Internal Revenue Service?

- Do I have an ethical, knowledgeable CPA? If not, where can I find one?

- Am I protected with all the insurance coverage I need?

- Do I have an up-to-date Last Will and Testament? Does my partner?

- Do I need a prenuptial agreement with my future spouse?

- I've discovered my partner is depleting our joint accounts. What can I do to protect myself financially?

- My spouse and I always fight over how our money should be spent. What can I do to end the stressful bickering?

- I'm going through a nasty divorce. What do I have to do to protect myself financially?

- My partner and I are good friends. We're going through an amicable divorce. What do I have to do to protect myself financially?

- I'm in a new relationship and my new partner wants to open joint accounts, pool our money, and share a checkbook. Is that best for me? What can I expect if we do? If I decide to go ahead, which one of us should handle the bill-paying and control the checkbook?

- My brother-in-law wants me to invest in his new business in return for shares of stock. Should I? What kind of return will I get for my investment? Will I lose my investment? Can I afford to lose my investment? If not, how do I say no?

- I'm planning to make structural and cosmetic improvements in my home. Is this a good investment? Will I get a significant return for the improvements when I sell my home?

- How can I save money to be used in a financial emergency?

- How can I save money for college tuitions? Retirement?

- Will I ever win a lottery or any other contest where I receive unexpected income?

- I've just received a windfall! How can I best invest the money? Do I need the assistance of a financial advisor? Where can I find the best one for me?

Your Spirituality

- What are the names of my Angels? Why are they working with me? How long will they be with me? Are they happy working with me?

- Do they have suggestions/ideas/recommendations for me?

- How can I best improve my ability to communicate with my Angels?

- What are the issues I chose for this lifetime?

- Which issues have I completed?

- Which issues do I still need to resolve?

- Am I sabotaging myself in any way? Why do I always have to learn the hard way?

- How can I most easily resolve the issues I have left?

- Am I moving forward quickly enough?

- What is my life's work?

- How and when can I get into it?

- Where will the talent and ability come from for me to be successful in my life's work?

- What were my past lifetimes?

- Was I a man or a woman?

- In what countries did I live? In what period of history?

- What did I accomplish? What didn't I accomplish?

- What were my special talents and abilities?

- What issues have I carried over that I am working on now?

- Who in my lifetime now was with me in previous

lifetimes? What kind of relationships did we have?

- Why did I choose the parents and siblings I have now?
- How are their issues connected with mine?
- Is it possible to build better relationships with them?
- Why did my children choose me as a parent?
- What are my children's issues and life's work?
- Did my children come from a past lifetime that was especially harsh or traumatic?
- Am I doing all I can to fulfill my purpose with them?
- Am I accomplishing what I am supposed to for myself and for others in my life?
- What purpose(s) do I share with my current friends in this lifetime?
- What are the special gifts, talents, and abilities that I have now from past experiences?
- What are the animosities, fears, and anxieties that I have due to past experiences?
- Why am I having such vivid dreams? What do they mean?
- Why are my pets with me and what purpose do they serve?

Your Health

- Do I have any health conditions I need to be aware of?

- Do any members of my family have any health conditions I need to be aware of?

- What is the best treatment for my (their) condition?

- Do I (they) need surgery for the condition?

- Who should perform the surgery?

- How soon should I have the surgery?

- Where should the surgery be performed?

- How long will my recovery time be?

- What can be expected following the surgery?

- How much discomfort will I experience?

- What will happen if surgery is not performed?

- Would I be better off with pharmaceuticals or a more holistic approach to my condition?

- Will physical therapy be necessary?

- To lessen discomfort, should I choose pain medication, acupuncture, chiropractic medicine, or another therapy?

- What is the spiritual reason for having this health condition? Is it a wake-up call? What am I supposed to learn from the experience?

- How soon will the recovery take place? Will I recover?

- I've just been injured. How serious is my injury? Who would be the best physician to treat the injury?

- How can I heal most quickly?

- What is the spiritual reason behind the injury? Is it a wake-up call? What am I supposed to learn from the experience?

- I *know* I have a health problem, but my doctors

can't seem to pinpoint exactly what the problem is. What should I do?

- How can I ensure the greatest physical health for my body?

- I'm considering cosmetic plastic surgery. Would I be happy with the long-term results? Would I be happy with my surgeon? How quickly would I heal? What are the risks?

- Do I need to improve my eating habits? What changes should I make? What will happen to my physical health if I continue with my current eating habits?

- What exercise program would be most effective for me? Least effective? What time of day should I work out? And where?

- How can I most effectively reduce stress in my life?

- How can I recharge my batteries?

- How can I develop more physical energy?

- Do I need any vitamin supplements? Should I visit a nutritionist?

- How healthy is my pet?

CHAPTER FIVE

Building
Communication Skills

Developing a Productive Relationship

To communicate with your guardian Angels as quickly and productively as possible, you need to be aware of exactly how your Angels are going to work with you and what you will encounter as you develop your relationship with them.

I highly recommend that you consider setting "meetings" with your Angels by making a verbal commitment to them. Set aside a specific time to practice your channeling. Arranging a meeting with your Angels is just like setting a date to get together with a friend or business associate.

All you need to do to set up the meeting is to say, "Sam, [or whatever your Angel's name is], I'd like to schedule a meeting with you tomorrow at nine in the morning."

It's as simple as that. You always make the decisions as to when the meeting will take place based on your time schedule and what is most convenient for you. It doesn't matter to your Angels when you want to communicate with them because they are always available to you any time of the night or day.

When you make the commitment to channel at a specific time, I strongly recommend you prepare an organized list of questions that reflect current priorities to ensure the time is wisely spent.

Your Angels will not only provide detailed answers to the questions you ask, but will also furnish any additional information that is important for you to know.

You'll absolutely love the fact that your Angels present information to you in a very frank, direct, and candid way, without sugar-coating anything. They have too much respect for your maturity and enlightenment to be anything other than extremely honest when you ask them your questions.

It is the Angels' philosophy to support you as much as possible with encouraging words, but they'll be quick to employ their no-nonsense method of communication and tell you the truth about your husband Irving having an affair with the babysitter. Rest assured that your Angels will always "give it to you straight" rather than providing vague, unrealistically optimistic, or censored information calculated to protect your feelings.

As you build the two-way communication with your Angels, you'll see that they have a totally different sense of time than we do here on the physical plane. We measure time in seconds, minutes, hours, days, and weeks.

In heaven, there are no such guidelines in measuring time. While seventy years on this plane is a lifetime to us, it is a mere blink of an eye to beings on the spiritual plane.

Therefore, when we leave the spiritual plane to go to Earth for another physical lifetime, we are hardly missed by those in heaven before it is our time to return.

When you realize how differently your Angels view time, you'll understand why they always seem to pressure you with observations like: "Hurry and get that issue resolved"; "We're really surprised you haven't done such and such yet"; "What's taking you so long to accomplish so and so?"; and "Let's do it now, now, now!"

Remember that their sole purpose is to guide and direct you throughout your lifetime, and a great part of their responsibility is to make certain that you achieve everything on your spiritual to-do list. Our Angels are on their own spiritual time clock, and consider our lifetimes on the physical plane incredibly fleeting compared to the infinite time and space in heaven.

Because the physical and spiritual planes are ironically on such different time clocks, our Angels have a different idea of how long our growth should take. To us, it seems obvious that our Angels drive us to distraction by continually pressuring us to move forward. From our Angels' viewpoint, it must seem as though we are dim, plodding creatures who have to be pushed and prodded to accomplish anything!

Building the ability to channel with your Angels is very much like building a relationship with an exalted mentor and friend, and the communication between you will be determined by mutual convenience. Occasionally you will need to set boundaries with them, just as you would with a friend on the physical plane.

Whenever you feel too pressured by their enthusiastic urgings, or you feel hesitant to pass along their intuitive information to another person, understand that your feelings are valid and must be communicated to your Angels for your relationship to continue to yield significant results. It is very important that you speak to them as openly and honestly as they speak to you.

So, in spite of the fact that your guardian Angels are heavenly beings and have your best interests at heart, it is perfectly appropriate for you to maintain your free will and to make all of your own decisions. It is perfectly appropriate to say to your Angels, "No, I won't" or "No, I can't," at those times when you feel it necessary.

You are the one living the difficult life here on the physical plane. The issues yet to be resolved are yours, as is the responsibility to accomplish your life's work. Your guardian Angels are not assigned to you to dictate your behavior or make your decisions. Instead, they are a divine *mentoring and support system* available to guide and direct your decision making and forward movement.

When you do set boundaries with your Angels, they will not get angry or disgruntled or choose to abandon you, simply because you are exercising your free will. No matter how important they believe a spiritual task to be, they recognize that the final decision is ultimately yours in terms of when, if, and how you actually accomplish it. And you won't be accruing any negative karmic brownie points if you hesitate or refuse to do something your Angels recommend.

For example, if you neglect to set "meetings" with your Angels, and they continually wake you up in the middle of the night to give you information, you'll find yourself exhausted and less productive than if you'd gotten a full night's sleep. If you become frustrated with their nocturnal communication, tell them so, and ask for a "meeting" at a more convenient time for you.

Perhaps they have given you intuitive information that they'd like you to pass along to a friend or acquaintance and you feel awkward or uncomfortable doing so. Share these feelings with your Angels and they'll simply ask someone else to accomplish the task.

Or perhaps your Angels are relentlessly urging you to quicken your pace through a very stressful situation, and you feel aggravated by the additional pressure of their insistent "encouragement." Just respectfully ask them to cease and desist, and they will do so immediately.

Why Certain Angels are Temporary

In my Angel seminars, many people are curious about how long our Angels stay with us and if the same Angels continue to work with us throughout our lifetimes.

As long as we remain on the physical plane, we have the wonderful opportunity to get acquainted with numerous guardian Angels who are assigned to help us through our issues and direct us to our life's work.

Each Angel is assigned to work with us in a particular area of our life. While one Angel may be directing us with our employment, another may be helping us with our personal lives, while yet another may be assigned to help us raise our children.

The relationship we share with our Angels is remarkably close and constant, and as we build our awareness of them and our communication with them, we come to rely and depend on their guidance, counsel, and advice. They do not foster our dependence on them to make our decisions for us, but rather, they are in place to help strengthen our independence, empowerment, and risk-taking ability gained through confident decision making.

Each Angel works tirelessly to provide us with the support and encouragement that represents their direct purpose. When we resolve a certain issue or accomplish what they were helping us with, their work with us is finished. Then they move on to work with someone else who is beginning the journey that we have completed.

Although most Angels stay with us only for the time required for us to resolve a particular issue, there are times when an Angel chooses to remain with us throughout our life. Those guardian Angels oversee the work that the other Angels are performing and usually have very close bonds with us that were begun in past lifetimes.

Frequently, when I give a private channeling session in my office for a client, I receive intuitive information not only from their Angels, but often from a deceased friend or relative who is also advising or protecting the person. While the deceased friend or family member is not formally acting as a guardian Angel, he or she has just as definite a spiritual presence as an Angel. Often he or she chooses to be involved in the protection and well-being of the loved one for as long as the person remains here on the physical plane. Usually a client will already be aware of the ongoing presence of their deceased friend or relative and considers their spiritual companionship extremely comforting and supportive.

How do you know when you have a new Angel? I refer to this phenomenon as a "changing of the guard." If you practice building your channeling ability, you'll develop an incredibly close relationship with your Angels. They will continually make you aware of the status of your work with them and let you know how successfully you are moving forward, which is the indicator of how long you'll be with them. Long before they retire from working with you, they'll announce that your work is almost completed and their presence is no longer necessary.

I'm a very sentimental and emotional person, and initially, this "changing of the guard" phenomenon disturbed and depressed me. I didn't like the thought of becoming so close and emotionally attached to my Angels, just to have them move on to work with someone else. Then I'd be forced to begin a whole new relationship with another Angel.

I felt very reassured when I discovered that I'd have the opportunity to speak with my departing Angel anytime I wished, although our relationship would be on a different level than the Angel/student one we had previously. The relationship between you and your retired Angel will be more of a mutual friendship that may elevate the existing bond between you significantly.

I've learned that it's truly a joy to be introduced to a new guardian Angel who is excited and enthusiastic about working with you. Angels all have very different personalities just like we do here on the physical plane. It's a magnificent gift to have the opportunity to build another heart, mind, and soul relationship with a spiritually enlightened being who places your welfare and happiness above all else.

The Physical Manifestation of Angels

One of the most exciting events you may experience is the physical manifestation of heavenly beings.

It is quite possible for your guardian Angels or departed friends and family to make their spiritual presence known tangibly by physically appearing before you so you can see, hear, and feel them.

At my Angel seminars, so many people have shared their stories of special encounters with deceased loved ones that I'm convinced it's much more of a common occurrence than any of us realize.

The film industry has consistently recognized the existence of heavenly beings and has portrayed their interaction with the physical plane in a number of highly acclaimed films.

Three of my personal favorites are *The Ghost and Mrs. Muir,* featuring a young widow who receives Angelic guidance from a deceased ship captain; *A Christmas Carol,* which depicts the nocturnal visit of Scrooge's three guardian Angels; and *It's A Wonderful Life,* in which businessman George Bailey develops a newfound appreciation for the quality of his life through the intervention of Clarence, Angel second class.

When my Angels first revealed themselves to me in a tangible physical form, they appeared as real as any person here on the physical plane. That's why their presence was so startling to me at first. I couldn't seem to believe or accept that a spiritual being was actually taking physical form. I've learned that spiritual beings have just as real an existence as we do. It took several months of daily communication with my Angels to understand that I truly wasn't losing my sanity and that they were indeed sent from heaven to help me.

Now that I've learned how common it is to see, smell, hear, or touch a spiritual being, I'd be truly surprised if you didn't have a tangible encounter with one of your own guardian Angels or a departed loved one. The more open you are to the experience, the more enjoyable and exciting the visit will be.

If you haven't ever tangibly encountered your guardian Angels or a departed loved one, and you'd like to have the experience, it is certainly possible.

When you channel, simply ask your Angels or deceased loved ones to tangibly reveal themselves in a physical form. Your Angels will appear in the physical form they choose that most represents their personalities (male, female, younger, older, etc.), and your loved ones will appear to you as you remember them.

It is also quite possible for your guardian Angels or departed friends and family to make their spiritual presence known tangibly by moving and manipulating physical matter.

There was an excellent example of this in the film *Ghost,* in which the deceased husband Sam Rice learned to prove his spiritual existence to his widow by manipulating material items in their home.

Since I began my psychic practice, I have heard numerous accounts of people seeing objects move through the air, discovering pictures of loved ones unexpectedly turned facedown on tables, plants and flowers thriving in gardens that the day before had been empty and barren, and a host of other incidents that people believed with true conviction were indeed a sign from Uncle Harry or a guardian Angel.

Do I believe that a spiritual being can really move a physical item? Yes, of course I do, but I have to admit that because I'm a skeptic at heart, I have a hard time believing all the stories I hear.

The three incidents I'm going to share with you actually happened to me, and you can believe their authenticity.

The first incident I'll share with you happened when I was eighteen. I was attending Loyola University and one afternoon in late fall, I developed a terrible headache from my worry over poor test results in a class I was taking.

I decided to skip my last class and drive home. On my way home, all I could think about was taking some aspirin and lying down to get some relief from the headache.

My parents and brother were away on a short vacation and I was staying in the house alone. I pulled into the driveway, locked the car, and entered the house through the garage door. I threw my purse and keys on the kitchen table, kicked off my shoes, and impatiently padded up the stairs to find the bottle of aspirin in my parent's medicine cabinet.

As I climbed the stairs, I heard a familiar, but muffled noise. I couldn't immediately distinguish what it was or even determine its source, but I remember feeling very confused because I had been alone in the house for the past several days.

I reached the top of the stairs and immediately saw

the door to my parent's room was uncharacteristically closed. I knew it hadn't been left that way. I was becoming concerned, but a little voice kept reassuring me that everything was okay. The voice then urged me to open the bedroom door and go into the bathroom where I would find something for my headache.

When I opened the bedroom door, I found the source of the noise. Water was running! I quickly strode into my parents' bathroom.

To my astonishment, the cold water was running full force into the sink. Beside the sink lay two aspirin and a clean glass. I then heard the little voice explain, "I wanted to help ease your headache."

The next incident occurred quite a few years later when I had already started my psychic practice. Early one morning, I ushered a female client into my office for a private channeling session. We sat comfortably and I started the tape recorder. She quickly discussed her priorities, which focused mainly on her relationship with her boyfriend.

When I began to channel about the relationship, I received the Angelic information that her boyfriend was just getting ready to propose marriage on her upcoming birthday and that she'd be very happy with him as a husband.

My client was naturally very pleased and excited, and then asked about whether they would have children together.

At that moment, another Angel broke into the conversation and began to communicate to me.

"Kim, I need to share a serious matter with her. Stop discussing the relationship."

I hadn't yet relayed everything to my client that the other Angel had said, so I continued to discuss the status of the personal relationship with her.

"Kim! Stop! I need to tell her something!" demanded the Angel.

"I will!" I responded telepathically. "Just let me finish—"

"No! Stop right now, or I'll turn off the recording device!"

I had every intention of providing my client with the information from the second Angel, but I simply wanted to finish communicating what the first Angel had said, and then move on to the other topic.

"I'll turn off the device!" he warned again.

Although I was fully aware that Angels have the power to communicate with us, I had a hard time believing a spiritual being could manipulate physical matter like my tape recorder.

Suddenly, and with no other warning, the machine loudly clicked off. My client looked at me in surprise, unaware of the silent conversation going on between me and her second Angel.

"Our time can't be over already," she observed.

"No, it isn't," I answered, noting that we were only fifteen minutes into the hour session. I picked up the machine to look for a technical malfunction.

"You won't find anything wrong with the machine," said the second Angel. "Will you stop being so stubborn and allow me to provide the information I wish her to have? As soon as you do, the machine will click on again."

I examined the machine and then I studied the tape. Both seemed perfect. I also thought to check the cord. It was firmly plugged into the socket. The Angel spoke again.

"Kim, as soon as you allow me to give you the message I wish her to have, the machine will turn on immediately."

Still highly skeptical about his ability to affect physical matter, and frustrated about the breakdown of my usually dependable machine, I agreed to put Angel number one "on hold" until I passed along the message from Angel number two. I realized that any time a heavenly being says a message is important, it is really important.

I told my client that another Angel needed to pass important information along to her about a different matter, and she was very agreeable.

"Thank you," said the Angel to me, and with that, he began to explain in detail what she needed to do that evening to protect herself during a very likely home invasion.

The Angel warned about a paroled felon who had been lurking in the neighborhood searching for victims. He had seen my client as she returned home from work the previous evening and had plans to break into her home in the middle of the night to sexually assault her. The felon knew enough about committing violent crime to wear a ski mask so she couldn't see his face, latex gloves so as not to leave behind telltale fingerprints, and a condom so as not to leave any traces of body fluids needed for successful DNA testing. He may never have been apprehended for his terrible crime because my client would have been helpless to identify him.

Her Angel told her not to go home that evening and to sleep at a friend's house. The next day after work she returned home with some inexpensive security alarms for her doors and windows that could be found in a neighborhood hardware store. In addition, her brother stayed with her until the threat was over and the parolee had moved on. The Angel had intervened during the reading to help protect the safety of my client who would never have known about the danger she was facing until it was much too late.

The third incident is my favorite to share because it is so fantastic that I know it sounds unbelievable.

Several years ago on New Year's Eve, I had been asked to make an appearance on a television program to discuss my psychic predictions for the upcoming year. It was a cold, blustery, rainy day and I was lucky to find a parking space right in front of the television station. I grabbed my briefcase and purse from the passenger seat, opened my umbrella, got out of the car, and hurried into the building.

I was on the program for a full hour, and was very pleased because it had gone so well. I stayed to talk for a moment with the host, whom I knew from previous appearances, and we talked about our respective social plans for the evening. After our chat, I retrieved my briefcase, purse, and umbrella and headed for the lobby.

Once in the lobby, I put everything down to search through my purse for my keys. They were nowhere to be found. I took everything out of my handbag, but to no avail. The keys were not there. In desperation, I also searched my briefcase and inside the pockets of my suit jacket. No sign of the missing keys. I began to get really upset because I only had one set of keys for my apartment, my office, and my car, and they were all on the one missing key ring.

To make matters worse, my car security system automatically locks all four doors immediately after I've left the vehicle.

Suddenly, I remembered exactly where I left my keys. I had thrown them on the passenger seat while I gathered my briefcase and my purse, and I never picked them up again! My keys were securely locked *inside* the car.

In total frustration, I looked at my watch and panicked. I was due shortly at another station across town. What would I do? How could I possibly explain this blunder to the two hosts of a television program who had focused the entire show around my appearance? That I've locked my keys in the car? It was like a bad psychic joke.

I quickly decided I had no choice but to go to the expense of taking a cab and I'd worry about the key situation later that afternoon. Then I heard one of my Angels suggest, "Kim, why don't you go out to your car?"

"What do you mean, go out to my car?" I argued telepathically. "To stand in the rain? My keys are locked inside!"

"Kim, go out to your car," she said patiently. "We know you left your key ring on the passenger seat and we've already taken care of everything."

"What do you mean, 'taken care of everything'? Do you realize what I've done? I don't have time to talk to you now! I've got to call a cab—"

"*Kim* Go out to your car! *Now!* We've taken care of everything!"

Although I couldn't fathom what they could do to possibly help me, I fully trusted them and knew my welfare was their highest priority. Feeling stupid and helpless, I grabbed my purse and briefcase, opened the umbrella, and left the television station.

"Look at the back of your car," the Angel instructed.

Having no idea what she was talking about, I peered through the cold rain and thought for a moment that my eyes were deceiving me. Exhaust was coming out of the tailpipe. My car was running!

"We're warming it up for you," she softly announced.

"But my keys were left on the seat!"

"We know. You have to be more careful about that in the future."

In total disbelief, I reached my car, but then hesitated. I knew the door would be locked, and if I pulled too strongly on the handle the piercing alarm would be triggered.

"Go ahead and open the door," the Angel encouraged.

"But I know it's locked."

"It was, but we've opened it for you."

"But how—"

"Kim! Get in your car! Now! Or You'll be late for your next television appearance!"

Her voice bellowing like a drill sergeant, the Angel startled me into action. I gently tugged at the door handle, and just like she promised, it opened immediately. The piercing alarm did not go off. I climbed into the warm car and found my keys inserted securely in the ignition.

Communicating With a Deceased Loved One

If you have lost someone close to you, please allow me to offer my heartfelt sympathies. I have lost several loved ones and I understand how you must be suffering through your grieving process.

I personally believe that once a loved one moves to the spiritual plane, our lives are forever and irrevocably changed and we have no choice but to accept and adapt to the loss here on the physical plane.

It is enormously difficult to suddenly be forced to live without the warmth, love, and tenderness of a close relationship. The loss is significantly more traumatic and harder to understand if it came as the result of an accident, a violent crime, or a wasting illness.

Similarly, many people are surprised to find how traumatic it is to lose a friend or relative with whom they did not share a positive relationship. They find themselves seriously haunted by guilt because they did not attempt to express their feelings, or resolve personal issues with the deceased, and have now lost any future opportunity to do so.

Communicating with a deceased loved one is the most emotionally charged kind of channeling and it takes a great deal of strength and courage.

Although we all belong to the same universe and our deceased loved ones remain close at hand and are readily available to communicate with us, our relationship with them is dramatically altered once they return to the spiritual plane. Because they permanently discard their physical body, we can no longer share physical interaction.

We must work to build new relationships with our loved ones in their new existence as spiritual beings. We can do this by developing our channeling skills and taking comfort in the knowledge that our loved ones are still accessible to us and can remain a part of our lives.

In fact, our deceased loved ones usually have no intention of abandoning or forgetting us simply because they have moved to the spiritual plane. Most often, they have a tremendous instinct to protect, support, comfort, and love us.

Once you begin to practice channeling, you'll become increasingly sensitive to their undeniable spiritual presence, which will allow you the opportunity, if you so desire, to actually hear their voices and "see" them again in a tangible physical form.

I am frequently asked to channel with a client's deceased loved one to convey certain information to them and receive messages from them.

In my work as a channel, I communicate back and forth between my client and their guardian Angels. Frequently my client is unaware of exactly who their guardian Angels are, so I introduce them by name and explain why each Angel is working with them.

However, when I receive a request to channel a client's deceased loved one, I ask for the name of the deceased, approximate age at death, and the cause of death as written on the death certificate. This information allows me to "page" the person I wish to speak with on the other plane and differentiates that person from any other.

When the deceased joins my client and me, they immediately begin to share the information they wish me to communicate to their loved one.

At times, the deceased complains that they expend tremendous amounts of energy in an attempt to make their spiritual presence known to those still here on the physical plane, but to no avail. Their grieving loved ones are too emotionally closed or too unfamiliar with the process of channeling to be able to perceive their spiritual energy.

One very interesting dynamic in this type of channeling occurs when a client pointedly asks the deceased to repeat something very personal that only the two of them knew about. Sometimes the deceased feels pressured for time, knowing we only have an hour for the private channeled session in my office.

He may have what he considers more important information to reveal, other than sharing a romantic nickname, or what he gave her for Christmas the previous year.

This situation is beautifully portrayed in the film *Ghost,* when channeler Ida Mae Brown tried to relate the message "I love you" from deceased Sam Rice to his widow, who suspiciously responded, "Sam would have never said that." Perhaps he never would have said it when he was alive, but he is certainly saying it now!

For example, how many times have you looked forward to a conversation with a friend because you had something important to discuss, and discovered that they felt what they had to say was more important, and you had a hard time getting a word in edgewise?

You could very well encounter the same situation when you channel with a deceased loved one. You may have certain topics you wish to discuss and you may discover that they have another agenda entirely. I strongly recommend that when you channel, you defer to them, because most likely, what they have to say will be very important. Remember, they are on the spiritual plane and are privy to much more intuitive information than you are.

I had an actual session with a client and her deceased husband that went like this:

Client: "Prove to me that it's really you, Harold."

Deceased: "I love and miss you, honey. Listen, I'm worried about you collecting my life insurance. The insurance company is trying to cheat you—"

Client: "Harold, tell me what you always used to say right before we went to bed—"

Deceased: "Muriel, please, listen. The insurance

papers are in the upper right hand drawer of my bureau. Find them and bring them to Sol, the attorney we had dinner with right before my heart attack—"

Client: "But Harold, how do I know it's really you? What did we fight about right before you had your heart attack?"

Deceased: "And honey, please give my beige lambskin overcoat to your brother, Tom. He'll need it this winter. They don't know it yet, but he and Shirley are moving to Idaho. His company is going to transfer him—"

Client: "Harold! Prove to me that it's really you! Where do I have that birthmark you always liked?"

Deceased: "Jesus, Muriel, listen to me, please! I never told you because I wanted it to be a surprise— look in the closet for my blue tweed jacket. In the inside pocket you'll find a bank statement. I opened a special account and was saving to take you to France. Please use that money to pay off the car. You haven't made the payment in two months and I'm worried—"

Client: "Harold! I can see that nothing's changed! It's so typical of you never to listen to anything I have to say . . ."

As soon as you have determined that you are emotionally ready to resume communication with a loved one who now exists on the other plane, you'll use the same channeling techniques as you would to speak with your guardian Angels.

The process is very simple. On a sheet of paper, write the name of the deceased, his or her approximate age at death, and if you know it, the cause of death as listed on his or her death certificate. If you don't have all of this information, write down what you do know. The vital statistics that you are noting will help "page" your loved one from anywhere in the universe.

As soon as your loved one joins you, he or she will begin to communicate and provide information to you by the same method as used by your Angels.

You'll be receiving information from your loved one by knowingness, hearing their voices, or by visual imagery that you "see" in your mind's eye, as explained in detail in Chapter Four.

The following is a list of the questions that are asked most often by my clients when we channel with a deceased friend or family member. Once you begin the communication with your loved one, you may want to ask one or all of the following questions:

- Are you okay now?

- What was it like to discard your physical body?

- Did you like your funeral service?

- What do you want me to do with your personal belongings?

- Since you didn't have a will, there is significant fighting among the family. What do you want done with your estate?

- What was it like to travel to the other plane?

- How do you like heaven?

- Is it as wonderful as everyone says?

- Where are you living on the other plane?

- What does your home look like?

- Who are you living with?

- How do you spend your time?

- What is your new life's work?

- Do you ever look in on me? When?
- How can I be more sensitive to your spiritual presence?
- Will you appear tangibly before me so I can see you?
- Have you seen Aunt Hannah (or any other deceased friends or family)?
- Did you accomplish everything you wanted when you were here on the physical plane?
- Will you still be in heaven when I get there in years to come, or will you have already moved on to another lifetime here on the physical plane?
- If so, do you know when you'll be coming back here to the physical plane and where you'll live?
- Will you and I have another lifetime together?
- Are you now one of my guardian Angels?
- Is there anything you wish to tell me?
- Is there anything you wish to tell the children, your parents, best friend, etc.?

CHAPTER SIX

Developing Self-Awareness

No Such Thing as Coincidence

Are you aware that everything happens in your life for a very specific and important reason?

There is no such thing as coincidence in the universe because everything that occurs in your life is a valuable learning experience to help you mature, gain wisdom, and develop spiritual enlightenment.

If you've ever heard yourself say, "I'm so unlucky!" or "Just as I get one problem solved, another one takes its place!" or "Why is everything always happening to me?", you're missing the point!

For example, you keep coming back to the physical plane lifetime after lifetime to fulfill two distinct responsibilities.

First, you have a life's work to accomplish. Second, you have issues to resolve.

Issues represent the entire fabric of human experience. All human beings begin their first lifetime on the physical plane with the very same number of issues to resolve.

Therefore we all have the same hardships, challenges, and difficulties to work through in order to evolve as a spiritual and contributing human being.

Our Angels remain right beside us offering guidance and protection, overseeing all the issues we are forced to encounter and attempt to resolve. If we are open to their communication with us, Angels have the ability to help make our progress far less painful, confusing, and time-consuming.

Why do we have to personally experience all of our issues? Why can't we develop instant awareness or enlightenment from our Angels, a textbook, or through the experience of other people?

With each successive lifetime here on the physical plane, we have the opportunity to resolve them all. Once we have resolved all of our issues, we reach the highest levels of enlightenment and no longer have to return to the physical plane. We may remain in heaven for all eternity.

Even though we may believe ourselves to be very sensitive to other people's feelings, we can't truly understand how a particular condition or situation feels unless we have encountered it firsthand.

For example, while ice skating at a local rink one afternoon, you break your tailbone. After experiencing significant pain and discomfort for several months, you finally begin to heal. Then you hear that your brother-in-law fell off a ladder while painting his house and broke his back. You can easily relate to his suffering because you experienced a similar injury. You know what he is going through and you feel a tremendous sympathy and compassion for him.

Or just after you and your husband move, a violent thunderstorm spawns a tornado that blows the roof off your new home. Although insurance fully reimburses you for the damage, you have continuing nightmares about the experience. While watching television a year later, you see a news story about a tornado that devastated a small town. You completely understand what those people are going through. Instead of dismissing their hardship because they are strangers, you feel a kinship with them fueled by tremendous sympathy and compassion because they are fellow victims.

Or perhaps you've wanted to start your own business for many years. You finally decide to go ahead and open your widget factory, and it becomes very successful. You feel tremendous emotional fulfillment just knowing you provide employment for hundreds of people. You enjoy the mental stimulation that comes from successfully competing in a challenging business environment. You fine-tune your decision-making ability. You develop complete financial security that provides a lavish retirement lifestyle, along with the opportunity to give significant sums of money to charity. Then you read about another woman in *Money* magazine who has accomplished a similar feat and you know the satisfaction and accomplishment she feels because you have met and achieved the same professional goals.

Maybe you and your husband have heard from friends what it is like to be pregnant, go through labor and delivery, and raise a child. You listen to their stories and share in their happiness. The day finally comes when you discover you are pregnant. You and your husband experience the pregnancy, the labor and delivery, and begin to raise your child together. Now you really know what the experience of childbearing is all about, only because the two of you have personally experienced it.

Although each human being starts his or her first lifetime on the physical plane with the same number of issues to resolve, the speed with which we resolve them is determined by our strength, awareness, and courage to face our challenges head-on without sweeping them under the rug or sinking into patterns of denial.

While we are still in heaven and before we embark on a new lifetime on the physical plane, we decide for ourselves which specific issues will be targeted for resolution. The issues we decide to work through will determine the identity of our parents and siblings, the economic background of our family, the part of the world in which we'll live, and whether we'll be male or female.

After all of those decisions have been made, we then choose other significant people to interact with, including close friends, spouses, long-term business partners, and important teachers and mentors, many of whom we've known before in previous lifetimes.

The reason we must choose all the people with whom we'll interact is because the people in our lives give us the wonderful opportunity to work through our issues. We select those individuals who will offer us the best possible learning experiences, and will quickly and effectively teach us what we've come here to learn in each lifetime.

Very often, we have to learn about the different forms of human experience through a difficult experience. We tend to learn fastest when we are in an uncomfortable, disagreeable, or disturbing situation. That's why we sometimes choose particularly difficult people to interact with, whose issues dovetail with our own. We learn fastest from them and the relationships with them become the most spiritually valuable.

For example, imagine you had an abusive parent who constantly criticized you and predicted you'd never amount to anything. You grew up hearing this relentless barrage of disapproval and came to believe that what your parent was saying about you was the truth. You developed a series of ''negative tapes'' that would play in your head long after you left home, reminding you of how insignificant and worthless you were.

You then choose a spouse who continues with virtually the same abuse you suffered at the hands of your parent.

Upon learning that we choose our parents, you might ask, ''Why would I choose an abusive father/mother? Who would choose such a home life?''

Choosing your parent was no coincidence. You chose the abusive parent to provide you with a valuable learning experience. You had the opportunity to learn about self-worth, self-esteem, and setting boundaries with your abusive parent. If you hadn't completely finished the work and resolved those issues by the time you left home as a young adult, you might unconsciously choose a critical or similarly abusive partner to help you finish the work you started with your parent. Your choices were strictly based on who could best help you work through the issues you were to resolve in this lifetime.

Do you always have to learn the hard way? Does life have to be a series of difficult, traumatic learning experiences one right after the other? Absolutely not!

We have the opportunity to resolve our issues in a much easier, faster way and to avoid a large part of the struggle and emotional pain. The faster we become aware of our issues and work to resolve them, the faster we'll move out of the emotional pain.

The type of childhood we had was no accident. We chose our family to help us resolve issues and evolve spiritually.

The type of marriage we have is no accident. We chose our partner to help us resolve issues and evolve spiritually.

The type of work we do is no accident. We chose our work to help us resolve issues and evolve spiritually.

The condition of our physical bodies is no accident. We choose past, present, and future health conditions/ailments to help us resolve issues and evolve spiritually.

If your car breaks down, it is not merely a huge inconvenience. It happens for a reason. If you win the lottery, it isn't simply a gigantic stroke of good fortune. It happens for a reason. If you receive a telephone call from a friend you haven't heard from in years, there is a necessary purpose for the conversation. It happens for a reason. If you lose your job, it isn't meant to ruin your life. There is simply something better for you elsewhere. It happens for a reason. If you break your leg skiing, it isn't a matter of clumsiness or bad luck. It happens for a reason.

Everything that happens in your life happens for a reason. There is no such thing as a coincidence or accident in the universe.

Since every occurrence or situation you encounter happens for a very good spiritual reason, make the decision to recognize the learning experience it offers, and work through the situation as quickly as possible.

To help you further understand there are no coincidences, I recommend that you utilize the following agenda as a tool to help you come into greater awareness of the reasons behind future problems and challenges:

1. Learn what issues you decided to work through in this lifetime by asking your Angels. Ask them which issues, if any, you have already resolved, and which are still to be resolved in the future.

2. Once you build an awareness of your issues, you'll start to recognize why you chose to have relationships with the people in your life, and how they provide the necessary learning experiences to help you resolve particular issues.

3. When you encounter a difficult or unexpected situation, understand that it is happening for a very good reason. Instead of asking "Why is this happening to me?", and wasting your precious energy in anger or frustration, refocus your question to, "What am I supposed to learn from this?"

If you address each new stumbling block in this way, no matter how large or how small the problem, you'll have an immediate understanding of why a particular problem is occurring, and most importantly, you'll have the resources to find solutions faster than ever before. If you subscribe to the "blessing in disguise" philosophy and believe that everything happens in your life to your best advantage, you'll be developing a brand new, very productive tool with which to work through your issues faster and with dramatically less pain. You will no longer have to learn everything the hard way!

The Wake-up Call

What happens if you don't decide to subscribe to the "no such thing as a coincidence" theory and find yourself regularly plunged into never-ending patterns of desperate longing, hideous confusion, and unproductive, emotional wheel-spinning?

What happens if you remain unaware of the issues you are meant to resolve or if you neglect to reach an awareness of your life's work?

You are likely to receive a *wake-up call,* which is a no-nonsense call to action orchestrated by your Angels to help move you forward, akin to being spiritually hit over the head with a heavy iron skillet.

Through the intervention of a wake-up call, we are given a necessary catalyst that occurs as a clear, concise event or series of events, unmistakably changing our lives and ultimately helping us create a better quality of life for ourselves and others.

Quite often, a wake-up call happens when we've reached the necessary levels of experience, wisdom, and enlightenment to accomplish an important spiritual task, but we lack awareness of what we are meant to accomplish and must have a catalyst to awaken us to our purpose.

When we receive a wake-up call, it provides not only a catalyst to awaken us to a spiritual purpose, but it also provides the energy to tirelessly pursue the special purpose we are meant to accomplish.

People who have directly experienced a wake-up call are all around us. We often hear them describe their catalyst as an initially negative or unexpected event such as an injury, illness, or the loss of a job.

The unexpected event, such as the loss of a job,

although traumatic at first, was created as a wake-up call to refocus the individual forward to a much more satisfying career path, perhaps to finally start his or her own business.

A wake-up call is an event that takes place in order to refocus our attention on a task we never would have been aware of or considered otherwise. It provides an emotional catalyst that drives us to accomplish the special purpose that we were born to achieve.

After experiencing a wake-up call, our Angels help us rally through the ordeal, as difficult as it may be. We become much stronger, more determined, and more aware than we ever would have been without the catalyst.

For example, a person who faced a serious illness decided to refocus his attention. He became an activist, fighting for more generous benefits from insurance companies and saving others the frustration he encountered.

Experiencing a temporarily disabling injury allowed another person the time to reflect upon difficult childhood issues and write a book about healing.

Our time on the physical plane is very limited and what we are able to accomplish is dependent upon how wisely we spend our valuable time, energy, and resources.

It is of vital importance that we achieve as much as possible while we are here on the physical plane in terms of performing our life's work and resolving as many issues as possible.

The universe will provide a wake-up call only if we remain unaware of our special purpose, and intervention is necessary to get us moving forward productively. A wake-up call could literally be described as a push forward, as you would lift the arm of a phonograph needle that has gotten stuck in a groove of a record.

In the early twentieth century, a woman lost her foster sister to suicide after the sister discovered that she was an illegitimate child. Years later, the woman married and gave birth to a son whom she lost in a tragic accident while he was still a small child.

These two traumatic incidents represent the unmistakable wake-up calls that inspired Edna Gladney to establish the Texas Children's Home and Aid Society, from which she placed over two thousand children with adoptive families. In addition, she successfully argued before the Texas state legislature to have the word "illegitimate" removed from all official records.

Timing Is Everything

After you have enough insight to question why something difficult or unexpected has occurred in your life, you must also ask why it happened when it did.

There are no coincidences in the universe in terms of why something has occurred, nor are there any coincidences in terms of when the event has taken place.

Your awareness of timing plays a crucial role in your success in every aspect of your life. To ensure greatest success, the universe will not allow any personal or professional opportunity to become available to you before the timing is perfect.

One of the most frustrating aspects of our existence on the physical plane is developing the patience required to work toward long-awaited personal and professional goals with discipline and resolute determination.

Quite often, we feel more than ready for a particular opportunity to present itself and yet we are forced to wait until a time our Angels have determined is best for us.

This happens frequently for clients who have private sessions in my office and receive the information from their Angels that their Mr./Ms. Wonderful will not be coming into their lives for several years.

Clients look crestfallen when I pass along the intuitive information that they have to wait for what they consider an inordinate amount of time to meet their significant other. They usually respond with, ''But I'm ready for him/her right now!''

If that were truly the best time, he or she would be already in the picture! A good question to ask your Angels would be, ''why isn't this the right time? Why do I have to wait?''

I always find it fascinating and informative to learn why my client has to wait. It could be that the significant other is still married and has to go through a divorce. It could be that the significant other has a current problem with commitment, and the universe doesn't want any potential setbacks. It could be that the significant other is struggling financially and is determined to hold off on a serious relationship until he can provide handsomely for a wife. The waiting period could also involve an issue my client is having a difficult time resolving.

When I share the reason for the delay with my client, he or she is reassured and usually very understanding. Most prefer to wait until the potential significant other has fully resolved the issues or dilemma that was causing the delay.

The universe will wait to bring the significant other into your life at the most advantageous time for the two of you to have the greatest possible success with the relationship. Once we learn the reason behind the necessary delay, it makes the waiting period so much easier and understandable.

Steven Spielberg responded to a question posed by the media about to why it took him so long to create and produce his film about the Holocaust. He explained, "If I had made *Schindler's List* ten years ago, I would have ruined it."

How can you make timing work to your advantage? Through channeling with your Angels, become aware of all the issues you have yet to resolve in this lifetime and try your hardest to address them, work them through, and heal from them. If you feel you might need professional therapy to help resolve your issues, then by all means, run, don't walk, to the best therapist you can find.

If you consistently work to face your challenges by asking, "What am I supposed to learn from this?" you won't be holding up the process of resolving issues and completing spiritual tasks. You'll be allowing and encouraging the universe to speed the timing involved in bringing before you all the opportunities you desire.

At times, we may be surprised by an unexpected opportunity that presents itself. We must remember that the universe never offers any opportunity to us before we are fully capable and spiritually ready to accept it.

When unexpected opportunities present themselves, however suddenly, it is imperative that we rise to the occasion to meet them.

Opportunities that we have not anticipated or

worked toward can often go unrecognized when they "fall into our laps" because we spend so much of our time and energy focusing on the other opportunities that we're trying to bring into reality. At times, our greatest opportunities come about when we are planning and working toward something else entirely.

There are times when we can fully recognize an unexpected opportunity when it is presented to us, but we lack the confidence to move forward, or we lack the energy or the desire to follow through.

For instance, my Angels repeatedly asked me to host seminars to teach clients how to do their own channeling. Over a three-year period, my Angels urged me to take advantage of these opportunities, but because of my shyness and fear of public speaking, I hesitated. Finally they convinced me to hold the Angel seminars by arguing that the lectures represented an integral part of my life's work. Although the "opportunity" to speak in front of a room full of people was totally unexpected, I've risen to the occasion to teach a great number of people to communicate with their guardian Angels, which in turn fills me with a tremendous sense of reward, fulfillment, and satisfaction.

What happens with timing when we don't take advantage of opportunities, whether expected or unexpected? We lose the opportunities.

There is a window of time that is allocated to us, and during this time we must begin to take advantage of the opportunity, or it passes to someone else.

For example, a man unexpectedly meets a woman who is his soul mate, which presents him with the opportunity for a heart, mind, body, and soul relationship that is meant to culminate in a wonderful marriage. At the time, he was unaware of the magnificent, singular opportunity the universe was presenting to him. Although he recognized her as a soul mate, he hesitated so much in moving their dating relationship toward marriage that he lost her in the process. He allowed the window of time given to him to secure the relationship to expire, and the opportunity of marrying the wonderful woman was presented to someone else.

As we gain greater awareness of the importance timing plays in the opportunities presented to us, we experience far more success in our pursuit of happiness and fulfillment.

How to Manifest

To manifest is to bring into reality that which we most desire for ourselves or for others, whether it is an event that we wish to take place, an opportunity we want made available, or the financial abundance we require to help us obtain material belongings.

It is our responsibility to directly communicate our dreams and aspirations to our guardian Angels when we channel, and provide them with the awareness of exactly what we are trying to achieve so they can work behind the scenes and help speed our progress.

A very important element in the process of manifesting is to include your Angels in the development of your goals. If you are trying to manifest something that is simply not meant to be, no matter how hard you work, your efforts at manifesting will be unsuccessful. Your Angels can help you set realistic guidelines so that your energy is wisely invested.

The kind of goals we may bring into reality

through the process of manifesting is unlimited, including those that represent our emotional, physical, spiritual, mental, and financial essentials. We have the opportunity to communicate our needs by channeling alone in our living room, or as a member of a group whose efforts in manifesting may likely bring about great changes for its participants or for those outside the group. We have the wonderful opportunity to manifest for ourselves and also for those whom we love and care for.

We may manifest to help others build a better quality of life free from illness, injury, addictions, dysfunction, poverty, and spiritual ignorance.

Manifesting was first introduced to me a number of years ago when I was starting my psychic practice. I had met another ''metaphysician'' for lunch and she complained that her car was getting more and more undependable. She told me about her plans to get a new car, and she was going to begin the manifesting process in order to receive it.

I had no earthly idea what she was talking about, so I asked her to explain. When she described the process to me, I found it very difficult to believe. With my typical skepticism, I chalked it up to a ridiculous waste of precious time and energy, although at the time, I was too polite to tell her so.

The next time I saw her, she casually mentioned her new car and how she came to acquire it just like she expected through the process of manifesting. She then indicated that she had fine-tuned her ability to manifest, and was doing so to achieve whatever she desired.

Her success piqued my curiosity, but I was confused about several points.

It was my understanding that our guardian Angels

were in place only to help us perform exalted spiritual tasks. It had never occurred to me to discuss anything so materialistic as acquiring a car or other material objects with them.

I also found it difficult to believe that I could get what I desired most not only with hard work, but by "putting energy into the universe," by communicating what I wanted to my Angels.

Manifesting sounded terrific in theory, so I decided to keep an open mind and test the theory in practice.

Since that time, I have had great success in communicating my desires to my Angels and I have been able to manifest many opportunities, including running a productive business in which I fulfill my life's work, becoming an ongoing member of a radio talk show, buying a new car, and even writing this book!

Because I'm a big believer in sharing, I have passed along the simple but very effective technique I have developed to clients who report that they too have yielded spectacular results.

If you follow my instructions, you'll be successfully bringing into reality that which you most desire!

The whole theory of manifesting revolves around communicating that which you most desire to your Angels. This process may take some practice for you at first, especially if you are not a very accomplished communicator.

All you need to do is tell your Angels exactly what you want in the most specific terms you possibly can.

Before you channel with your Angels to manifest, be certain to make decisions about what you want, why you want it, when you want it, and when discussing material items, what type, kind, or color you most desire.

It is very important to write down all of your specific preferences to keep you organized and focused on your goals. This will allow your Angels to understand exactly what you are trying to communicate.

For example, you might wish to manifest a business opportunity. Before you speak with your Angels, this is what you should write:

I want to start my own business because it is part of my life's work to be an entrepreneur, and a business of my own will give me the opportunity to offer employment to others. I want to manufacture bicycle pumps and sell them in my own store and also through a catalog. I want my first store to open within the next year. (Give specific date.) I believe I will need twenty thousand dollars in start-up capital which I need my Angels' help to manifest.

Or, if like my friend, you wish to manifest a new car, this is what you should write to your Angels:

I want a new car because my existing car is undependable. I would like a new forest-green Honda. (Give specific model and year.) I want the new car in the next ninety days. (Give specific date.) I will need a three-thousand-dollar down payment which I need my Angels' help to manifest.

You may wish to manifest a significant other. Before you speak with your Angels, this is what you should write:

I want a Mr./Ms. Wonderful to share a heart, mind, body, and soul relationship because I am now ready for a commitment. I would like him/her to come into my life this summer. (Give specific time or date.) I would like to be married by this time next year. (Give specific date. You must also list the internal and external qualities you wish him/her to have.)

What has happened when you set your goals, and manifest like crazy, but to no avail? You've made one of two common blunders. First, you may have forgotten to ask your Angels whether or not a situation you desire would be for your best benefit. Second, you may have disregarded an important dynamic communicated to you by your Angels.

Perhaps one of your goals is to develop a relationship with the new man in your apartment building. You're very excited about the chemistry you feel when you see him and you begin to manifest the opportunity for you to meet and go out together. Months go by and he hasn't asked you out for so much as a cup of coffee. Out of frustration, you channel with your Angels, and ask them why you can't seem to manifest this opportunity. They explain that this man is not a Mr. Wonderful for you and that if you did somehow build a relationship with him, you'd be miserable. In trying to manifest a going-nowhere relationship, you'd be completely wasting your time.

Let's say you absolutely hate your job and have your heart set on starting your own business. You have previously channeled and your Angels confirmed that you are meant to be an entrepreneur. You start a widget factory and manifest daily for its success. But your widget company does very poorly. Out of frustration, you channel once again with your Angels and ask them why you weren't successful with the business. They explain that although you were certainly meant to have your own business, you ignored their instructions about starting a printing company and instead opted to invest your time, energy, and resources into widgets. No matter how hard you worked building the widget company, you are meant to do something else that would bring you far more fulfillment, satisfaction, and financial rewards.

Don't waste your precious time and energy in denial, stubbornly trying to manifest something that is not the best choice or opportunity for you. The only time you'll have trouble manifesting is when you are concentrating on a person, place, or thing that would ultimately not bring you happiness. If you are unsuccessful in your attempts to manifest, it means there is someone or something much better for you waiting in the wings. All you have to do is ask your Angels for greater guidance and you'll be destined to reach success with whatever you attempt to manifest.

After you have channeled with your Angels and have verbally communicated what you wish to have their help in manifesting, you are to review your written goals every day for a minute or so, to reaffirm that you remain serious about achieving or acquiring what you desire.

Remember, as you develop your written list, be realistic with your time frames. Leave your Angels a little elbow room in which to work behind the scenes to help you. Even they may find it impossible to help you manifest something as quickly as four o'clock this afternoon, or by midday tomorrow!

CHAPTER SEVEN

Discovering
Your Personal History

The Soul's Memory Bank

There are two distinct sources of intuitive information. Intuitive information comes directly from our Angels through the process of channeling. The other source of intuitive awareness is the soul, which is inside every human being.

When I conduct a channeled session for a client, I can often psychically "see" their soul as a tangible organ located right behind the heart. In some readings, I actually access information both from their Angels and also from inside their soul's memory bank.

The soul is the only part of us that survives whether we are on the physical plane where we are now, or in heaven after the physical body expires. Although we alternate from the male to the female gender, and we have very different personalities in each of our physical lifetimes, our souls perpetually endure the transitional process as we travel back and forth from the physical plane to the spiritual plane.

During each of our lifetimes on the physical plane, we incorporate, or add, every experience we encounter. All the knowledge acquired from resolved issues goes into the soul's memory bank. So in each successive lifetime, we come back to the physical plane carrying greater and greater wisdom, maturity, and enlightenment gained from all the lifetimes before.

Our souls are one of our greatest gifts from God, because they hold the records of our personal histories throughout our lifetimes. It is very much like a spiritual photo album that is available for us to review at any time to help us "remember" who we are, where we've been, and where we're going in each lifetime on the physical plane.

What is the difference between the guidance available from our Angels through the process of channeling and the information that we access from our soul's memory bank?

The soul's memory bank is a rich source of intuitive information providing the road map, or itinerary for this lifetime. Our Angels help us accomplish what is on our spiritual itinerary by giving us directions, advice, and helping us consistently measure our progress.

The soul carries in it vast stores of information, much like a computer disk. This fascinating, insightful information is available to you at any time and includes all of your personal history from each of your past lifetimes. Without the knowledge and awareness of your past life experience, you remain in spiritual amnesia. The soul is an open book that will allow you to discover hidden assets and other essential facets of self-awareness which will prove invaluable in your ability to achieve emotional, spiritual, physical, and financial growth and security.

How can you access information from your soul's memory bank?

Retrieving information from your personal "file" is incredibly easy. Like channeling, you've had the ability to access your soul's memory from the time you were a child, although you may have remained unaware of the process.

As I said earlier, the soul is located in the human body just behind the heart. Although it may not be visible to the naked eye, it may be "seen" physically as a tangible organ. The soul performs the vitally important function of relaying intuitive, spiritual information to you to help and assist with all of your decision making.

It is fully programmed with all of your prior experiences from past lifetimes and your unique talents and abilities. It is a record of all the decisions you made before your rebirth to the physical plane for this lifetime, including your life's work, your issues, and the identity of the special person who is to be your soul mate.

Your soul's purpose is to help you forge a pathway in each lifetime that will lead to accomplishment, self-awareness, and spiritual enlightenment. The soul achieves this by sharing with you all the information that makes up your personal history.

The soul is positioned just behind the heart because it releases information to you through what you feel emotionally. You access information from your soul every time you feel.

As human beings we employ two distinct methods of making decisions as we go about our daily lives. The first method is to think about what we're going to do with analytical, left brain pondering before we make a decision. This usually requires quite a bit of time because, in my opinion, the brain is one of the slowest organs in the body. The brain is also the source of all of our negative tapes that run so inconveniently, just as we're trying to make an important decision.

For example, you've been offered a new job. You begin your decision making using the brain's thought processes and immediately your negative tapes begin to play: "I'm not good enough or smart enough for the new job"; "What if the new boss doesn't like me?"; "I hate my current job, but I know it's secure . . ."

The brain renders you incapable of making truly wise decisions because it is the source of the negative tapes that play over and over in your head, scaring and disabling you. Worse, it is not privy to any intuitive information at all.

The other method we use to make decisions is to *feel*, or use our instincts. We feel our way to an answer or a solution. When we feel, we come to decisions very quickly, spontaneously, and with more confidence. We hear no negative tapes coming from the heart as we do from the head.

Instead, what we hear coming from the heart is actually the soul releasing supportive, encouraging information to us, on an as-needed basis, allowing ease and confidence in the decision-making process.

You'll be accessing soul information if you make your decisions with your feelings instead of what your head tells you to do. To increase the information you receive from your soul, you must live your life through your feelings.

For example, a person who is exclusively a *thinker*

will receive very little soul information. A *feeler* can access any and all of the information inside his or her soul simply by regularly acting upon his or her feelings.

Accessing soul information could be compared to the process of weight lifting. Like the soul, you have the muscles already in place within your body. When you begin to lift weights, you'll start out slowly, building an awareness of your physical body, just as you'll build an awareness of your emotional body as you use your feelings.

In a short amount of time, you'll be very familiar with your physical body and what it's telling you about how capable you are in terms of building muscle. You'll just as easily recognize what the soul is telling you you're capable of to achieve greatest happiness, peace, and contentment.

The soul works on an as-needed basis. It will release only small amounts of information until more is emotionally requested. The dilemma thinkers' experience is the ongoing battle between what their heads tell them to do and what their souls are trying to tell them through their feelings.

Every time you act upon your feelings, you send a request to your soul to release more information to you. The more you request soul information through acting upon your feelings, the greater the amount of information it will make available to you. You'll increase the trickle of soul information released to a flood of ongoing knowledge and awareness by turning off the thought processes and developing the emotional body.

Now that you are familiar with the process of accessing soul information, it is important for you to understand everything contained in your soul's memory bank.

The Complete Dossier
of Your Past Lifetimes

Our soul is a truly amazing organ. It has the capacity to hold an infinite amount of information, but unlike a computer, never shuts down, loses input, refuses to retrieve vital data, or becomes obsolete.

Just how many past lifetimes they have actually lived is a matter of great curiosity to a number of my clients. They ask, "Have I had any? I'm not sure, but I think I've had several."

What I normally discover from accessing the information from their souls is that they've had *thousands* of past lifetimes. This is true for the majority of people I have seen in my office and it probably holds true for you.

Take out a pen and sheet of paper and jot down your thoughts on the following topics. This is a very worthwhile exercise to help you discover just how much you are actually moving forward. Focus for a moment on the last five years of your life.

1. What obstacles or hardships did you encounter?
2. What did you learn from these hardships?
3. What did you learn from the other people in your life?
4. What did you learn about the other people in your life?
5. What issues did you resolve?

6. What opportunities did you create and/or take advantage of?

7. Did the last five years redirect your goals and desires? If so, how?

8. What were the situations or experiences that you didn't expect?

9. How have your philosophies, thoughts, opinions, and feelings about life changed because of what you have experienced?

10. What have you discovered about yourself in the last five years?

I refer to this exercise as "soul searching" because it provides you with a focused, tangible awareness of how much your life has actually changed and shifted over the relatively short period of five years. My life changes so rapidly that I usually perform this exercise every year on my birthday, to help me remember how much I have accomplished, to help me concentrate on how much I have learned about myself and others, and to help me discover where I might have fallen short of reaching my goals.

Now that you have performed this exercise, you're probably amazed to see how much the last five years have affected the way you think and feel about yourself, the way you view the other people in your life, and how remarkably you've changed your goals, desires, and direction.

Your continued spiritual and emotional growth will be easily recognizable by performing my "soul searching" exercise to allow you the awareness of just how much and how quickly you are evolving.

In keeping with what you have discovered about your evolvement over the last five years, just imagine how much growth and development will take place over the course of an entire lifetime.

Then visualize how extensive your spiritual and emotional development has become over the course of thousands of lifetimes and you'll be coming to an understanding of how much information is contained and readily available from your soul's memory bank.

You should be curious about your past lifetimes because they represent your personal history. You may access past lifetime information from your soul's memory bank that includes the period in which you lived, where you lived, whether you were male or female, and if you shared a previous lifetime with any of the same people who are currently a part of your life.

Accessing information about past lifetimes from your soul is a fascinating experience, almost like watching the movie of the week. It is very much like viewing a video on television in that you can actually jump into it and have the ability to see, hear, smell, feel, and actually be a part of the past as you once lived it. You'll also have the wonderful opportunity to "see" people with whom you shared a prior lifetime and who are very much a part of your life now.

I know it sounds silly, but I once was afraid that if I "went back" to a past lifetime, I'd somehow get stuck there and wouldn't be able to return to my current life. I've learned since that it's impossible to remain in the past lifetime, even if I wanted to.

When we regress, or visit, one of our past lifetimes, we are only accessing a memory of what existed before from the file our soul maintains. Our trips into past lifetimes, as real and vivid as they may appear, are nothing more than spiritual memories of the past. Although Angels can provide past life information, it's very fascinating to receive past life memories from the soul because we have the opportunity to personally go back and observe what has taken place, rather than just hearing about it from our Angels.

To access past lifetime memories, choose a quiet environment where you won't be disturbed. You may want to sit in a chair rather than lie down, because if you get too comfortable, you might drift off to sleep!

Close your eyes and tell your soul that you wish your past lifetime file opened. If you already have an intuitive awareness of a particular past lifetime, you might ask your soul to start your past life regression in that period of time.

In your mind's eye, picture a staircase in front of you leading up to a bright blue door. On the other side of the blue door is one of your past lifetimes. Picture yourself slowly climbing each stair, and as you do so, tell yourself that you're becoming more and more relaxed.

When you reach the top of the stairs, slowly open the blue door, cross over the threshold, and walk back into a past lifetime.

While you are there, realize that the images you "see" are being made available by your soul because they hold the key of awareness for you now, to help you find a solution to a problem, clear up existing confusion, or help you make a decision about a pending opportunity.

Each time you ask your soul to access your past lifetime files, you may return to the same lifetime you've already visited or you may visit another lifetime entirely.

Don't be frustrated or disappointed if you keep regressing back to the same past lifetime. Keep in mind that your soul is trying to provide you with necessary intuitive information and will continue to present a vision of the same lifetime until you have reached an awareness or understanding of its significance. If you've tried unsuccessfully to interpret the information your soul is providing to you, remember that you can always ask your Angels for help and guidance.

Your first few attempts to retrieve your past lifetime file may seem confusing as your ability to access information grows. You'll probably "see" small bits and pieces of a past lifetime and your vision may appear cloudy at first. With practice, you'll develop your ability to see clear and vivid images of your past lifetimes provided by your soul's memory bank.

Your Hidden Gifts, Talents, and Abilities

As you access information from your soul about past lifetimes, you'll also come into an awareness of your hidden gifts, talents, and abilities.

I refer to these endowments and levels of expertise as "hidden" because most people have no clue whatsoever how accomplished they are.

I've had nationally known surgeons, famous actors, elected officials who hold high political offices, successful entrepreneurs, and critically acclaimed writers and artists disclose in their private channeled sessions that they have no idea what gifts or abilities they possess. In all seriousness, they ask me to channel with their Angels to find out whether they have any special or unique talents at all!

It is extremely important to focus on gifts, talents, and abilities that we had in past lifetimes. If we remain ignorant of what we have achieved in the past, we have no real idea of who we are or where we are in the present, which renders us helpless to make appropriate decisions about where we are capable of going in the future.

If you receive information from your soul that you'd be a fine writer because you have written in a past lifetime, trust that. If your soul tells you that you are meant to be an entrepreneur because you have prior experience from a past lifetime, by all means start your own business!

By pessimistically exclaiming, "I can't!" or "I've never done that before!" or "I have no experience!" or "I never thought I could do that!" or "If I have that talent, then why don't I know it and how come I'm not already doing it?" You will only slow down your progress in achieving what you truly desire. Be open to the wonderful wealth of information your soul is releasing to you.

In other words, do you remember riding a bicycle as a child? If a friend asked you to go bike riding this Saturday morning, you'd remember the experience you had as a child and feel confidence in your ability, even if it has been many years since you've last ridden.

Maybe last summer you helped a friend build a brick patio. Or you learned how to ride a horse. Or you went out on a date. Or learned the breaststroke in a backyard pool.

If you thought about attempting any of these activities again you wouldn't be disabled by anxiety or insecurity because you'd remember your prior experience. Even if it wasn't a great experience, you'd still be aware that it was an accomplishment. There would be no fear of the unknown. You'd have the confidence of knowing you had prior experience.

It's the very same process with past life experience. If you've already accomplished something, the ability and talent is already there for you to access any time you desire.

In addition to channeling with your Angels, you'll also have the opportunity to access information about your talents, gifts, and abilities from your soul's memory bank to discover what you've already accomplished and achieved in past lifetimes.

For example, if you were an Olympic athlete in a previous lifetime, you'd be athletically gifted in all of your future lifetimes. If you were a farmer in a previous lifetime, you'd be gifted with the ability to raise livestock and successfully harvest crops in all of your future lifetimes. If you were a famous sharpshooter in the American Old West in a previous lifetime, you'd likely be very comfortable on a horse and have fine marksmanship skills in all of your future lifetimes.

Once we have developed a talent or ability, it remains with us as part of our soul's memory bank for all eternity. That's why we can attempt something that we have never tried before and excel at it so quickly. Rest assured that you've done it before in a past lifetime!

Your Current Fears and Anxieties

All of your current fears and anxieties can be traced to three distinct sources.

First, you may be experiencing psychic or clair-voyant images that are warning you about what is likely to happen in the near future.

Second, you may be worried needlessly about a situation that will never occur. This phenomena is simply "thinking too much" and I explain it in detail in Chapter Eight.

Third, your fears and anxieties that have past life-time origins.

How do you properly differentiate among the three? By channeling with your Angels.

I have found that almost all anxieties stem from past lifetimes. If you have a terrible fear of the water, you've very likely suffered the experience of drown-ing. If you have a fear of fire, or snakes, or flying, I guarantee that if you explore your past lifetimes through the information available from your soul, you'll discover that your fear isn't ridiculous or silly, but very appropriate and one that you'll need to con-centrate on healing and resolving. We can't heal from an issue until we learn exactly where the issue came from and how it began.

When I was a child, my family lived in close prox-imity to railroad tracks. I can recall lying in bed late at night and becoming overwhelmed with a terrible fear when the train would rumble through my neigh-borhood. I can vividly remember thinking, "All those poor people in there!"

I was also very confused as a child because I had a bone-chilling fright of ever traveling to Germany.

In addition, I had horrible nightmares about being locked up against my will. As the passenger of an automobile, I'd hyperventilate if we traveled any-where near a jail or prison.

I wondered where these feelings came from and I

was often bewildered about why I was the only member of my family to harbor these fears.

During my very first attempt to access information from my soul about past lives, I immediately found myself "seeing" clear images of my last lifetime, which was in France during World War II. In my last lifetime, as a child I was forced into a boxcar for the frightening journey to Bergen-Belsen concentration camp, where I was interned until my death from typhus.

Those past life images provided by my soul helped to clear my confusion and armed me with an awareness of exactly where my fears and anxieties were born.

Having the opportunity to physically "witness" what I had been forced to endure in that lifetime, it suddenly seemed perfectly natural that such fears would remain part of my psyche. I felt vindicated through my new understanding of the logical reasons behind my fear, and was then quickly able to heal and resolve those issues.

If you are seeking to resolve certain fears and anxieties of your own, and are not looking back into your past lifetime, you will be focusing on only a small portion of the problem. No matter how hard you work or how good your therapist, your fears may remain unresolved, because you'll be treating only the symptoms of your anxieties instead of productively treating the original cause.

Your Life's Work

The two biggest sources of spiritual frustration for most people are the lack of awareness of their existing talents, gifts, and abilities, and a general confusion about the nature of their life's work.

In addition to this information being readily available from your Angels, you'll also be delighted to know that your soul carries in it the vital information about the decisions you made just prior to this lifetime about your life's work.

Your soul's memory bank is programmed with exact information you'll be able to fully access in terms of how you are meant to get into your life's work, and in what time frame you will have the best opportunity to accomplish it.

Consider the fact that you specifically chose this particular period in time to be on the physical plane. The life's work you decided upon reflects those opportunities that are available now in this day and time.

For example, the life's work you would have chosen had you lived during the time of the French Revolution, or during the American Civil War would have certainly been very different than what you have chosen for yourself in this lifetime.

If you are a woman, certain kinds of life's work would have been strictly off limits to you. Think about how much greater your choices and opportunities are now than they were just thirty or forty years ago.

Most people dramatically limit the scope of what they think they can accomplish because they remain totally ignorant of their talents, gifts, and abilities. Once you access that information from your soul, you'll have a much better outlook and level of confidence to achieve all that your life's work entails.

How can you access information from your soul

about your life's work? Ask yourself what your feelings are telling you. What are your dreams?

Perhaps you've always dreamed of owning a health care clinic, or being an attorney, a chef, or a massage therapist.

How do you know if you are not currently in your life's work? Are you unhappy, bored, unfulfilled, unstimulated, unchallenged, and not earning a proper living? If so, you can assume that you have to retrieve some information from your Angels or from your soul's memory bank to discover exactly what your life's work really is.

Your soul will tell you what occupation would make you happiest and allow you to contribute most to others by flooding your heart with feelings.

If you are a thinker and are having a terrible time accessing your feelings, the following exercise will help you become more sensitive to the information your soul is trying to provide to you. It is an excellent method of soul-searching even for the most "mental." After you've completed the exercise, you'll have a specific awareness of your life's work!

What career path would you choose if:

• you had to work?

• you had only one year left to live?

• you had to make a positive difference in another person's life by performing a necessary service or providing a necessary product?

• no matter what career choice you made, you wouldn't fail?

• start-up capital was readily available?

- you'd be supported emotionally with your career choice by family and friends?
- you'd have guaranteed financial security?
- you'd reach emotional, mental, and financial fulfillment?

Your Unresolved Issues

Besides achieving your life's work, the resolution of our issues is the primary reason we keep returning to the physical plane.

We can certainly ask our Angels about the issues we are meant to resolve, but we may also access information about the challenges we face in this lifetime from the soul's memory bank.

Some issues are so difficult, we naturally hesitate before addressing them. Substantial issues may commonly span several lifetimes until we are successful in resolving them.

If we explore the history of an issue through our soul's memory of past lifetimes, we may then come into an awareness of how to efficiently heal and resolve it without creating any additional pain or suffering.

The Identity of a Mr./Ms. Wonderful

Before we are reborn into each lifetime, we decide who will make the most exceptional partner for us, with whom we'd have the opportunity to enjoy a heart, mind, body, and soul relationship.

A soul mate type of union is different from any

other in that it is a gift to us from the universe. Once we have found our soul mate, we no longer have to experience the difficult "learning experiences" that are so much a part of less enlightened relationships.

The Angels always describe meeting a soul mate as a monumental, life-changing event and one that we realize is tremendously important the moment it occurs because of the feelings it inspires.

How do we recognize a Mr. or Ms. Wonderful? How do we spiritually remember who we chose to spend our lives with? How do we learn to differentiate between that one person and all the other men or women in the universe?

Have you ever heard someone speaking about the first time they met their soul mate? They commonly describe the event as "Incredible! I knew I would marry him the first moment I saw him!" or "I knew she would be my wife on our first date."

Soul mate relationships move forward faster than any other, because in their hearts, both partners quickly recognize the other as the one they are meant to share their lives with in peace, harmony, and fulfillment. You will feel your Mr. or Ms. Wonderful the moment you meet him or her because your soul will provide you with an unmistakable knowledge and awareness.

The Purpose
of Your Current Relationships

Each one of the people we encounter has a distinct purpose in our lives and is very likely someone with whom we've shared a previous lifetime.

How can you become more sensitive to people who have been in your life before?

Have you ever had the experience of meeting someone who you immediately liked and felt affection for, and you intuitively recognized that you somehow knew them? You experienced a reunion with someone with whom you shared a very positive past life.

Have you ever had the experience of meeting someone whom you immediately disliked and who repulsed you? You experienced another type of reunion, but this time, it was with someone from a past lifetime with whom your prior encounters were difficult or traumatic.

It is crucially important that we develop our ability to recognize the purpose that every person is supposed to play in our lives.

While still in heaven, we reach a mutual decision with the people who we plan to interact with on the physical plane long before we're reborn into each lifetime.

Therefore, we carry a spiritual responsibility to ourselves and the other people in our lives to recognize the kind of relationship we are meant to have with them and to honor and fulfill our spiritual promises.

How can we recognize the role other people are to play in our lives? We must make our decision as to how we are going to proceed with each person we meet by listening to the information our soul is providing us through our feelings.

Channeling and Religion

The first time someone has a private channeled session in my office, they frequently ask about my spiritual convictions and if I believe in God. They also ask me to explain the differences, if any, between religion and spirituality.

As a child, I was raised as a Catholic and took part in weekly catechism for many years. As a young adult, I attended Loyola University, which is a Catholic college that prides itself on encouraging students to develop and strengthen their religious beliefs.

I now consider myself a "recovering" Catholic, not because of any particular animosity toward the religion itself, but because my growing enlightenment has opened inspiring new doors and helped me widen my horizons, and the strict doctrine of the Catholic church no longer fills my spiritual needs.

What follows are my personal opinions which I have developed from my extensive work with Angels and my growing familiarity and daily contact with the spiritual plane. My opinions are meant to explain and clarify, rather than convince and convert you to my religious or spiritual beliefs.

While it is very important to stay open to new ideas and philosophies, it is essential to maintain your beliefs no matter how much anyone tries to convince you otherwise. I feel that adults must decide for themselves what they believe and how they are going to pursue their beliefs. I also have come to acknowledge that each one of us has a different view of God, our Angels, and the universe because we are all so unique in our past life histories and our varying levels of enlightenment.

In terms of my personal spiritual philosophies, I have an unshakable belief that there is one God in the universe, whom the Angels sometimes refer to as "the white light."

I have also developed a devout reverence and a

profound faith in the thousands of Angels I have channeled who express unconditional love and selfless commitment to those of us they support, guide, and protect here on the physical plane.

Prayer is one of our most important daily activities and we pray every time we communicate with our Angels through the process of channeling.

We don't need the presence of a priest, rabbi, or minister to allow us to talk to God or our Angels, nor do we have to be in a church, temple, or other house of worship to do so. We have the wonderful opportunity to pray at any time and in any environment of our choosing.

Religion is the embodiment of organized faith, where people come together for the purpose of praying and to share and observe the particular beliefs of that faith. In many organized religions, people are encouraged to seek advice and instruction from religious leaders to help them work through difficult issues and to help them become closer to God.

Spirituality is the embodiment of individually observing and pursuing beliefs without restrictions and regulations of religious dogma or doctrine. Individuals seek direct guidance from God, their Angels, and their souls when seeking solutions, guidance, and advice.

Can a person embrace both spirituality and religion at the same time? Of course! Spirituality and religion are similar in that they both attempt to teach the basic principles of right and wrong, offering behaviorial guidelines for the way we conduct our lives and the way we interact with other people.

Whether we as individuals choose to embrace independent spirituality or an organized form of religion, or a combination of both, observing and upholding these valuable teachings are critically important to our continued growth and spiritual evolution.

How do you decide what philosophy to embrace? How can you best develop your spiritual or religious beliefs to best suit your lifestyle and represent your growing enlightenment?

Experiment with different religions by attending services and meeting members of the congregation. Are the other people who attend the services individuals you would describe as "kindred spirits"? Did they welcome you to the services, or did they regard you with unfriendly or hostile suspicion? Did you enjoy and feel uplifted by the services?

Explore the development of your spirituality through regularly attending lectures and seminars about spirituality that will widen your horizons and open new doors for you. Make friends with others who are seeking to develop their level of enlightenment.

A wealth of reading matter and tapes can be found in religious or metaphysical bookstores. If you research and explore what they have to offer, it will help you decide which philosophies you feel most comfortable in embracing.

If you decide to explore what is available to you in terms of an organized religion, be wary of certain red flags that will immediately indicate that the religion is not for you and will only stymie your growth and limit you. The red flags are as follows:

- Does the religion purposely inspire feelings of fear, guilt, and shame?

- Does the religion warn its congregation to close

themselves to new or different ideas that are outside their religious doctrine?

* Does the religion encourage its congregation to harbor suspicions about other people simply because they don't belong to their church?

* Does attending the religious service make you feel miserable, hateful, or depressed, instead of uplifted, inspired, and encouraged?

* Does the religion teach prejudice, hatred, or a judgmental philosophy toward others?

* Do the clergypeople or members of the congregation of the religion try to force their philosophies onto others and convert or "save" people who do not subscribe to their beliefs?

CHAPTER EIGHT

Building a Beautiful Life

Paralysis Through Analysis

How would you best define your basic philosophy of making decisions, problem-solving and interacting in your relationships with other people?

Although you may feel both philosophies somewhat apply to you, would you describe yourself more as, "I think therefore I am," or "I feel therefore I am?"

The answer to that question greatly determines your ability to channel with your Angels as well as your ability to access your creativity, spontaneity, intuitiveness, risk-taking capability, and confidence in decision making.

How can you identify whether you are a thinker or a feeler?

If you operate more from the mental center, which is the "seat" of logical, rational, analytical, thinking impulses, you are more of a thinker.

If you operate more from the emotional center, which is the "seat" of creative, intuitive, expressive, feeling impulses, you are more of a feeler.

For example, let's explore the differences between the way thinkers and feelers respond to life and other people.

Risk-taking

Situation: You've just been offered the job of your dreams at a salary three times higher than what you are currently earning. The offer requires that you relocate to another state where you have fantasized about moving to for years.

Thinker: "Oh my God! I never thought that this would happen! What a decision! Well, let's not be hasty. I know I'm not earning what I should be, but my current job is secure. I could stay at my present job until the day I retire. What if I don't like the new company? What if they don't like me? What if my boss becomes disappointed with my performance? I might be fired! I also have to consider the move. I'm bored and unhappy with where I'm living, but my rent is reasonable and probably won't go up until next year. Moving out of state seems a bit drastic. What if the cost of living is much higher there? Is that why they offered me so much more money? What if I move there and don't really like it? What if I move there and don't make any friends? I'll have to think about this for a while. I'll sleep on it. I need time to weigh and analyze what the logical decision should be. The company will just have to wait a little longer for my decision ..."

Feeler: "Oh my god! I knew in my heart that this would happen! I knew I was the best person for the job. I'll be a great asset to them. I'm certain I'll love my new job! And I do deserve more money. I look forward to meeting my new co-workers, and my new boss. I can't wait to be more challenged at work. I've been so bored with my current job. And I've been bored with where I'm living. I've always dreamed of moving and living in a new environment. I'll have the opportunity to make new friends! The universe is really providing for me and helping me manifest my biggest goals! Its been thirty minutes since I talked with personnel. I'll call them right away to accept and start planning my move! I wonder how soon I can start . . .''

Relationships

Situation: You've finally met your soul mate and have been dating for some time. You sense the relationship is becoming serious and the topic of marriage is about to be discussed.

Thinker: ''Why does the relationship have to move so quickly? Are we in a race to get somewhere? My heart tells me to move forward, but my head tells me to wait and consider. There are too many things to think about. What if he really isn't the right person for me? I thought the relationship with Jim was right for me several years ago, but look how that turned out! My mother/best friend/business colleague tells me to wait because my soul mate isn't what they pictured for me. And I don't know if I can provide what the other person needs. When things become emotional, I get uncomfortable. What if he gets bored with me? What if I get bored with him? What if we fall out of love? What if our sex life diminishes?

There are so many divorces out there, I certainly don't want to be another statistic! And if we do divorce, what if he tries to squeeze me for money? He makes me happier than I've ever been and he is the most wonderful person I've ever known, but how can I be absolutely certain that I'd be doing the right thing? How can I be guaranteed that he is the best person out there for me? What if there is someone better? And what if we decide to have children? They are so expensive! What's wrong with the way things are? What's the big hurry? Why can't we keep the relationship just where it is for say ... well ... another three months ... or six months ..."

Feeler: "I can't wait for the relationship to move forward! We're both experienced adults who know what we want. We've had plenty of time to really get to know one another. And we both realize that we're soul mates! I've waited a lifetime for this kind of relationship! It makes all my awful prior relationships seem valuable and worthwhile, because now I have the awareness and enlightenment to tell the difference between a man who offers a hard learning experience and a man who is a real Mr. Wonderful! I love the thought of marriage with this person. I feel that we'd be very happy and I'm confident the relationship would last for the rest of our lives. It will be a matter of continuing to consider each other's feelings as a first priority. Our current relationship is so successful. We're so stimulated by each other. We have such great communication. And our sex life couldn't be better. We'd make such terrific parents! Raising children would be challenging, but I wouldn't feel my happiness was complete without them. I know he is in love with me and I'd never find anyone else who could make me feel as in love as I am right now. I know it because of what my feelings are telling me. I've never been so sure of anything in my life. I wonder what he would think about getting engaged and marrying next month . . .''

Channeling Ability

Situation: You've been practicing your ability to channel with your Angels and you have developed a tangible two-way communication with them.

Thinker: ''How can I be sure that it's actually my Angels speaking to me? Maybe this process doesn't really exist and I'm just kidding myself. It's probably all my own imagination. It can't be possible to communicate with Angelic beings who are in spirit form that I can't see, hear, or touch like a human being. If it were so easy, wouldn't everybody be aware of the process? Wouldn't everybody be channeling? Why should I work at something that I can't openly discuss with people? I can imagine the response I'd get from discussing channeling with my Aunt Martha/poker buddies/business acquaintances. And I'm not even sure if I know what my Angels are trying to tell me. I think they keep urging me to make decisions and move forward, but I don't like to react that quickly. I keep feeling that they're talking to me, but I try to ignore them because I don't always agree with what they're saying. I'm just too busy to listen. Maybe I don't really have any guardian Angels. If I did have Angels working with me, wouldn't my life be easier or happier than it is? I bet these rumblings aren't Angels talking to me. It's probably indigestion from all the cold pizza I've been eating . . .''

Feeler: "I'm really channeling! I'm so excited to be developing a relationship with my very own guardian Angels! They talk to me all the time. I'm going to work very hard to build my ability to communicate with them by setting time aside to practice my channeling. I'd love to be able to receive information for my mother/friend/acquaintance and pass it along to them to make their lives easier. I can't believe how much more information I can receive now that I couldn't pick up before. When I talk to them about a problem or a challenge or an opportunity, they make everything seem so understandable that I know exactly what to do! I wish I had developed my channeling ability years ago. I move forward so much faster now because I know what is ahead for me. Because of the intuitive information they give me, I never have an emotional rug pulled out from under me anymore. I see opportunities much more clearly, and I know exactly which learning experiences I can avoid, and how to get through the ones I have to encounter much faster. I enjoy sharing what I've learned about Angels and channeling with other people, even if they've never been exposed to the process before. It's made such a positive difference in my life. . . ."

Decision-making

Situation: You've just been informed by a trusted physician that minor surgery is required to remove a benign tumor that is growing rapidly under your arm.

Thinker: "I knew I'd need surgery! Dr. Smith probably isn't certain if the lump is cancerous and doesn't want to worry me, so that's why she told me it is benign. She probably won't know for sure until she removes it. I've been seeing her for years, but I wonder if she really knows what she's doing. I've always been afraid I'd get cancer. What if something goes wrong in surgery? What if she makes a terrible mistake and I die on the table? And I can't afford to take time off work if my recuperation takes longer than expected. What if my insurance refuses to pay the medical bills? What if my insurance company drops me? What if I contract AIDs during the surgery? I wonder if I should check public records to see if Dr. Smith has any malpractice suits filed against her? I can feel the tumor growing bigger every day and it's making me very uncomfortable to have this surgery hanging over my head, but I'm just not ready to follow Dr. Smith's advice to schedule the operation right away. I can't make that kind of a decision until I take some time to weigh and analyze everything that could go wrong ...''

Feeler: ''I knew my lump wasn't cancerous! What good news! My Angels said it was benign, but what a relief to get my intuitive information confirmed in a second opinion from Dr. Smith. She said the outpatient surgery will take less than an hour. I feel so fortunate! I'm so glad I have a doctor I trust. I know in my heart that she'll do a wonderful job in surgery and that I'll be in very good hands. I'll bet my recovery will go faster than expected because I heal very quickly. And when I'm at home recuperating, it will be the perfect time to catch up with my reading and write to old friends. I'll use this time to my advantage to rest and take good care of myself. The lump is getting bigger every day and makes me feel so uncomfortable that I'm going to take Dr. Smith's advice and schedule the surgery right away. I feel it's the right thing to do. Although the surgery is minor, I'll be happy and relieved to have it over . . ."

Do you see how differently thinkers and feelers respond to the same situation?

As a thinker, you will encounter difficulties in several areas that will continue until you further develop and fine-tune your feelings. Being the thinker that you are, this will not initially make sense to you. After all, you've been doing just fine up to now performing tasks, meeting and fulfilling obligations, and solving problems. Why is it necessary for you to change the way you respond to the challenges and opportunities that are presented to you?

Because if you remain a thinker, you're missing out on a lot of what life has to offer.

People who are thinkers, like the one described above who needed surgery, are usually chronic worriers who expend quite a bit of their precious time and energy worrying about problems and events that will *never* happen. They can drive the people around them to utter distraction as they become consumed in negative thought patterns and compulsively dwell on every hideous possibility of each situation or challenge they encounter, making any forward movement interminably painful and brooding.

In addition, thinkers are endlessly tormented by pessimistic thought patterns that I refer to as "negative tapes." Unexpected problems, difficulties, or opportunities trigger these negative tapes to start running, creating enormous fear and inner turmoil that cripple decision making and the ability to take risks.

As discussed in Chapter Seven, many of us have our own series of negative tapes that were originally created by our parents or other family members, friends, our first-grade spelling teacher, significant others, business associates, and anyone else we came in contact with who had criticism or negative things to say about us.

It's amazing how long these tapes play, and they continue to play relentlessly until we manage to get them erased by doing our healing. I have found that erasing negative tapes usually requires the help of a good therapist who can objectively direct your healing to make certain you get all of them erased, and as quickly as possible. If you don't get them erased, they'll play perpetually and negatively color every personal or professional relationship you ever have.

When faced with a challenge, the thinker immediately hears the negative tapes repeating: "I'm not good enough"; "I'll never fit in"; "They won't like me"; "I'm not smart enough"; and "I'll never amount to anything."

Thinkers can't help but be affected by their negative tapes because they hear them so often. They become so accustomed to hearing the negativity, that eventually they fully believe the taped criticism as if it were gospel.

The next time your negative tapes begin to play, notice how disabled and insecure you begin to feel. Negative tapes also create an incredible level of mental chatter and commotion that renders you helpless to access and hear your more subtle feelings.

In addition, the thinker in the above scenario who was wrestling with his/her decision about the soul mate relationship was experiencing the common dilemma that occurs when there is a power struggle between what our head is telling us to do, which is usually directly opposed to what our heart is trying to tell us.

Quite often when this situation occurs, thinkers decide to do nothing right away but sit back and wait for "time to take care of everything" or the hope that "it will all work out somehow."

When you decide not to make a decision and therefore do nothing, that is a decision to keep things status quo. Keep in mind that even if you don't act, you've still made a decision, and that decision is not to move forward.

Learn to Shut Off the Mental Chatter

While you are working to get your negative tapes erased and re-recorded with positive messages, I have a simple technique to help you turn off the negative tapes and shut down all the accompanying mental chatter. If you follow this technique, you'll immediately have the opportunity to access and actually hear your feelings.

When you hear your negative tapes begin to play, simply say aloud, "Shut off!" and wait to see if you're successful. If your brain continues to play the tapes, just repeat, "Shut off!" I normally have to instruct my brain to shut off at least twice before it will respond. I know it sounds ridiculous to talk to your brain, but it works!

How will you know if your brain has shut off? By the peace you feel internally. The mental silence will be deafening, especially if you're a true card-carrying thinker. Sit back and enjoy the new sensation of inner quiet, and listen for a moment to what your feelings have to tell you.

One of the most difficult and significant problems you'll encounter as a thinker is if you find yourself desiring a serious relationship with a feeler. You may become confused and disgruntled by the constant emotional demands made by your partner, and your partner may feel endlessly frustrated by what they perceive in you as a constipated level of emotional expression and affection.

If you're a thinker, perhaps now you can see why a little change might be in order to help improve the quality of your life. Why not begin right now to operate more from your emotional "seat"? You'll have absolutely nothing to lose and everything to gain!

You'll be shutting off your negative tapes, and learning a whole new way of looking at yourself and the world around you without the constant stream of old criticisms.

Your Angels will have a chance to finally reach you with vitally important intuitive information because they will no longer be drowned out by the roar of mental chatter and commotion.

Instead of having a tendency to make everything much more difficult than it has to be, you'll have the opportunity to develop more productive decision making that will allow you to act with more control in all areas of your life instead of feeling frightened or confused, which puts you in the uncomfortable position of always reacting to other people, problems, or challenges.

The personal relationships you develop will be far closer, warmer, and more satisfying than ever before because you will interact with the other person emotionally. If you only share your mental energy and physical body with your partner, then you are not fully sharing yourself with him. If you truly desire a heart, mind, body, and soul relationship, you'll have to open emotionally to your significant other and trust him with your budding vulnerability. It's the only way you'll truly bond romantically with another human being.

How can you successfully accomplish the metamorphosis from the mental "seat" to the emotional "seat"?

First of all, you must learn to quiet the mental chatter caused by your negative tapes by practicing the phrase, "Shut off!" until your brain responds.

After you have quieted the mental chatter, you need to begin to listen to your feelings. Expect to encounter some initial confusion as you learn to differentiate between what your brain tells you and what your heart tells you. A good rule of thumb is that the information you receive from your head will be negative and depressing, and the information you receive from your heart will be positive and uplifting.

Telltale signs you are being "mental" is when you say, "I think," "I know," or "I believe."

Refocus and look inward to learn what you are feeling. Try to incorporate phrases into your vocabulary like "I sense" or "I feel."

Pretend that you are breaking yourself of a bad habit, such as biting your fingernails. Every time you communicate, be wary of your tendency to be "mental." Refocus and look inward and ask yourself what you are *feeling*. Your determination and commitment to concentrate solely on what you are *feeling* is all that is necessary for the change to take place within you.

In a sense, by communicating emotionally, you'll be going through a similar process as you would learn a new language.

In the beginning, you'll be reminding yourself to speak your new language, which is *feeling,* rather than your old language, which is *thinking.* After you practice making emotional decisions and speaking from the heart, feeling will become second nature. Believe it or not, you'll be fully convinced after you experience the difference feeling will make in the quality of your life.

If you have "emotional" family members, friends or a significant other, it is a very good idea to involve them in your metamorphosis. Most likely, they'll be delighted to help you with your progress by providing emotional support and encouragement. They can also make you aware of those occasions when you slide back to your old "mental" way of communicating or decision making by observing, "You're doing it again!" just as they would if you were chewing your fingernails.

Once your Angels no longer have to compete with all the mental commotion, you'll be receiving more intuitive information than you ever thought possible. In addition to the help you receive from family and friends, if you rely on advice and counsel from your Angels, you'll move forward to become more "emotional" faster, and with greater confidence and security.

If you truly desire to evolve and to change old habits, it will take time, a little courage, and quite a bit of tenacity, but it is certainly within your grasp. You'll progress and successfully become a feeler who makes confident decisions, is comfortable with risk, enjoys spontaneity, is eager to channel, and enthusiastic about developing an emotionally bonded romantic relationship.

The Four Batteries in Your Body

Have you ever felt that your internal "batteries" were running low and you were coming close to mental, physical, or emotional burnout?

Or that you were bordering on exhaustion and knew you had to find a way to discontinue what you were doing until you could recharge?

If so, I applaud your intuitive awareness. The human body has four internal batteries that dictate levels of physical endurance, mental stamina, emotional energy, and spiritual awareness. They all operate independently and are responsible for enabling our bodies to survive and function productively.

Each battery has a limited supply of "juice" that we have to replenish when levels decrease and we start feeling fatigued as a result. As we participate in normal daily activities we are continually depleting our levels of energy, or juice, but our batteries have an infinite capacity to hold increasing levels of energy as we build our ability to produce and replenish it.

The Physical Battery

The physical battery is responsible for the level of energy in your physical body. We are all accustomed to the familiar sensation of feeling run down physically, and fatigue is an indication the juice in that battery is running low.

To replenish physical energy levels, you can eat, sleep, rest, soak in a hot tub, or even exercise.

The Mental Battery

The mental battery is responsible for maintaining levels of intellectual alertness and awareness. When you become mentally fatigued, your brain can no longer focus, concentrate, or perceive and filter information.

A clear signal that your mental juice is depleted is

when you find yourself repeatedly reading the same passage in a book or magazine without retaining or understanding the material.

To replenish mental energy levels, you have no choice but to discontinue whatever you were doing for the time it takes to recharge.

Once you reach mental burnout, it is quite common for a bad headache to ensue because the juice is drained and any further time you spend forcing yourself to complete a mental task will be counter-productively spent in frustration.

The levels of juice in your mental battery will rise as soon as you distance yourself from what you were doing intellectually and become involved in a physical, spiritual, or emotional pursuit.

The Spiritual Battery

The spiritual battery is responsible for our ability to channel with our Angels and other beings on the spiritual plane. When you first begin to channel, you will probably feel tired or even exhausted after about twenty or thirty minutes of communicating and you'll have no more energy to continue.

You'll discover that as you regularly practice your channeling, you'll be increasing the levels of juice available to you because you'll be expanding the capacity of the spiritual battery to hold energy.

The first few times I worked on my ability to channel, I got so exhausted, I had to take a nap! With practice and experience, I have built the available levels of "juice" in my spiritual battery to enable me to channel all day.

To replenish energy levels, you must simply stop channeling for several hours to allow the juice to be restored to former levels.

The Emotional Battery

The emotional battery is responsible for emotional balance, well-being, confidence, and optimism.

Clear signs that the emotional battery is running out of juice are when you feel depression, irritability, negativity, anger, or weepiness for no apparent or obvious reason. You may also experience restless sleeping patterns and problems with digestion or elimination.

Unlike the physical, mental, and spiritual batteries, the emotional battery is the only energy center in the human body that has to be manually recharged with juice. In other words, you cannot simply stop feeling and wait for the energy levels to return.

To replenish the emotional battery, you must plan events and activities to look forward to. The activities can be relatively small, as long as you enjoy the anticipation.

For example, the ways I recharge my emotional battery are eating Italian food, dancing to Billie Holiday, reading a new magazine, watching my favorite old movies, getting a massage or a facial, channeling for my family, exercising, going to the movies and the theater, and shopping.

How many times have you said to yourself, "I'm so depressed! I have absolutely nothing to look forward to but work, work, work!" Of course you're depressed! Who wouldn't be?

You have to create your own list of activities that will help you recharge. You can't rely or depend on anyone else to make wonderful plans for you, including your significant other. I've found that just doesn't happen. *You* have to assume responsibility to make your own plans to accomplish your emotional recharging.

Do you think I'm totally crazy to advise you to include such frivolous activities into your already overcommitted and ridiculously hectic schedule? *You can't afford not to take the time to recharge!*

I understand what you're probably feeling. When my Angels first told me how to recharge the emotional battery, I thought they had gone off the deep end. I couldn't believe they were asking me to incorporate playtime in my busy schedule. As an adult, my life had become very stressful and so full of issues and responsibilities that I came to believe playing and having fun was only for children.

I soon understood that when I started to feel depressed and emotionally exhausted for seemingly no apparent reason, I no longer needed to feel guilty. I learned that I was entitled to feel that way. I shared so much emotional energy with other people that my levels of juice naturally decreased, and I felt emotionally drained. By the end of each work week, I was so depressed from exhaustion that I wanted to throw myself off the top of a building.

I discovered that if I took just a little bit of time to recharge my battery with an activity I really enjoyed, my attitude became optimistic and positive again, and I was able to resume my task-related activities renewed and refreshed with a heightened level of emotional energy.

Channeling and the Physical Body

Your ability to channel will not only be determined by the level of juice in your spiritual battery, but also in how you ensure the vitality of your physical body.

In my opinion, fueling your body with junk food, fried food, caffeine, refined sugar, alcohol, any type of pork, too much red meat, sodium, or dairy products can actually sabotage your efforts to channel successfully no matter how long or how hard you practice.

While I was growing up, my mother used to affectionately refer to me as the Goodie Queen.

Unfortunately my unhealthy eating habits persisted, and when I first began to channel, I believed that refined sugar, carbonated beverages, chocolate, and dairy products represented the four major food groups! I couldn't understand why my physical energy levels always plunged late each morning and late each afternoon until I "recharged" with a diet soft drink, a candy bar, and something salty like pretzels. What a mistake! I was needlessly sapping my precious physical energy by eating junk that my system had to work twice as hard to digest.

After several hours of channeling for clients in my office, I regularly found myself so sick from exhaustion that I'd have to call to cancel the rest of my appointments. I was mystified by how my channeling energy disappeared so quickly each day. I finally asked my Angels about the problem and they told me I was not only draining all my channeling energy, but that I was ruining my health as well!

To safeguard my health and remain as "clear" a channel as possible, I gave up all forms of refined sugar (including chocolate!) red meat and pork, caffeine, sodium, most dairy products, carbonated beverages, and any type of fried or prepackaged foods. I also began to take the vitamins and minerals recommended by my Angels.

It wasn't easy, believe me, but I found that once I gave up the sugar, chocolate, and caffeine for several weeks, all my other hideous cravings for junk food virtually disappeared.

For the first time in my life, my energy levels went through the roof, my resistance to illness improved dramatically, I felt happy and energized all through the day, and my physical body responded with a new vigor to my normal daily activities. I was also able to shed the ten pounds that I couldn't seem to lose before I revamped my eating habits.

Are you wondering what I do eat? My new, healthy diet consists of fruits, vegetables, natural cereals, pasta, salads, chicken, fish, vegetable and fruit juices, a soy beverage I use on cereal, decaf coffee, and plenty of water. Once in a while I'll enjoy a glass of wine. And what do I eat now for a goodie? Sugar-free popsicles and sugar-free, fat-free yogurt. When I really need a "fix" I treat myself to my all-time favorite junk food that I still love to indulge in—movie popcorn. And not the air-popped variety that tastes like pieces of a styrofoam ice chest. I know it's loaded with fat and sodium, but it's the one junk food I simply won't give up.

Through trial and error, and with enormous persistence from my Angels, I continued to change my eating habits until I found the best dietary regimen for me.

What's best for you? Ask your Angels and your physician what they recommend in terms of your eating habits and whether you need vitamin or mineral supplements. Do not make any dramatic changes in diet or exercise without consulting your doctor! As you work through the process of revamping your eating habits, be certain to pay close attention to the way your physical body is responding to its new fuel.

You will also discover that your channeling ability will be enhanced through light, regular physical exercise including walking, swimming, weight lifting, aerobics, or any type of sports activity that you enjoy.

Getting enough sleep at night is also a must for you to access intuitive information from your Angels clearly and concisely. If your Angels begin to regularly interrupt your sleeping patterns, make an "appointment" with them for a more convenient time to allow you to get your much-needed rest.

There are a number of very beneficial New Age health treatments that are beginning to gain popularity.

One that I strongly recommend is the process of cleansing the spiritual energy of your body.

Did you know that people use sea salt to cleanse crystals? Sea salt can also be used to revitalize you if you're feeling particularly drained or fatigued and it can also boost the energy levels, or juice, in both your spiritual and emotional batteries.

Although you may find sea salt in some grocery stores you're sure to find it in a health food store. I also want you to be aware that you can't substitute table salt or rock salt for this type of cleansing.

Fill your bathtub with warm water and add three full cups of sea salt. Do not add soap or anything else to the water. This bath is for relaxation and energy cleansing only! Soak for at least twenty minutes. You may then rinse off the sea salt in a shower, but I personally like the feeling of it on my skin overnight.

Aromatherapy is another beneficial New Age health treatment that incorporates the therapeutic properties of plant and flower "essences" and oils to invigorate, rejuvenate, soothe, calm, and relax the human spirit. You'll be surprised to learn how many oils and essences are available, each with very distinct properties that you'll want to investigate and explore. Soaking in a hot tub with a delightful oil can have a phenomenal impact on your physical, mental, and emotional energy levels! Aromatherapy products can be found in almost any health food store or shop that sells metaphysical products and supplies.

The Best Time to Channel

How do you incorporate channeling into an already hectic schedule? Keep in mind that when you practice your channeling, all you'll really need is a brief ten to fifteen minutes. But you'll have to make the time, just as you would for exercise, dating, playing with your children, or other activities that are important to you. Remember, we can always find the time for our greatest priorities.

What time of day will you have the most energy to communicate with your Angels?

You'll have to experiment to find what time of day works best for you. Interestingly, it may not coincide with your internal clock.

For example, I am most definitely a night person. I feel terribly foggy and disgruntled when I have to get out of bed before six-thirty in the morning. I am most alert in the afternoon and I usually get another blast of energy around 9:00 p.m., and although I don't get the opportunity very often because of my schedule, I adore staying up late at night.

My strongest channeling energy, however, is during the day, from 9:00 a.m. to 6:00 p.m.! I couldn't channel late at night, even in an emergency, because my channeling battery starts to dramatically lose steam in the early evening.

Try to set aside fifteen minutes to practice your

channeling first thing in the morning to determine how much energy you have at that time to support the communication. Then on alternate days, attempt to practice at lunchtime, and late in the afternoon, and finally, try to channel in the evening. I guarantee, certain times will be far better for you than others in terms of your energy levels.

The Best Place to Channel

The best environment for you to channel in the beginning is definitely a quiet one where you won't be distracted by your spouse, children, the television, radio, or telephone. I've found soaking in a warm bath to be a very productive place to channel!

I strongly suggest you do not attempt to practice your channeling while driving. When I was first starting to channel with my Angels, I decided to begin a conversation with them while I was parked in front of a stop light. The light turned green, and I proceeded through the intersection. Suddenly, one of my Angels tangibly appeared in the seat next to me and I almost drove my car into a tree!

Noisy restaurants and other public places are also too distracting to practice your channeling, even if a friend or family member pleads, "But please, I only have one question!"

I would *never* channel for anyone in a public place unless the environment was very quiet because I want to be certain that I am receiving the Angelic information correctly and with the integrity in which it was provided to me.

CHAPTER NINE

You're Off and Running!

Practice Techniques

Now that you are communicating with your Angels, it's very important to practice your channeling skills. If you work regularly on channeling, you'll quickly discover how much more accurate your intuitive information will become. Accuracy of the information you receive is the primary foundation for all your Angelic communication.

In addition, you'll be surprised at how much more expanded and specific the information is that you'll be receiving, which is just as important to the quality and integrity of your readings as accuracy.

Whether you are channeling for yourself or for someone else, when you take the time and energy to talk with your Angels, you want to be certain that you have the ability to receive correct, specific information each time you communicate. Practicing will allow you to achieve a more significant, ongoing flow of intuitive information. As you work at channeling, your interpretive skills will also dramatically improve and you'll easily be able to access Angelic information of the highest caliber.

When you first start to channel, you'll find your confidence levels rather shaky. That's to be expected. Don't allow a meager level of confidence to slow you down, or worse, stop you in your tracks.

Remember, your Angels regularly speak with you whether you are aware of them or not, and they are very eager and enthusiastic communicators. That is their whole purpose in working with you. It is up to you to reopen your ability to fluently communicate with them. The more you practice your channeling, the greater your skills and confidence will become. I guarantee it!

Keep in mind that your ability to channel will be like riding a bicycle. You first learned to communicate with your Angels when you were a child, and so you already possess all the skills necessary to resume speaking with them. You'll simply be continuing a skill that you developed earlier in life.

The following recommendations are easy and enjoyable practice techniques that have evolved from my series of Angel seminars. These exercises have proven successful for a great number of people who have learned to recapture and develop their unique ability to communicate with their Angels. With a little practice, you will, too!

Predicting Sporting Events

Sporting events provide a perfect medium for practicing your channeling ability. You'll be able to check your accuracy as soon as each game is completed. Throughout the year, you'll have the opportunity to predict the outcome of professional athletics' that include football, baseball, basketball, soccer, hockey, and even golf tournaments.

Build your channeling ability by predicting which team will win a particular event. I strongly encourage you to write down the name of the two teams that are playing, the date they will play, and where they will play. Concentrate quietly for a moment and you'll receive Angelic information about which team will triumph. If you desire, you'll also be able to receive unlimited, more in-depth information about point spreads (of course, not for the purpose of gambling), individual players, their injuries, how they will perform in the game, and finally, the coaching staff.

As you first start to channel, don't frustrate yourself by trying to predict the outcome of the Superbowl or World Series at the start of the season. Wait until you are more seasoned and experienced to channel from a large group of team names. You may end up very confused or frustrated, and I want you to enjoy the exercise. Speaking of enjoying the exercise, it really doesn't matter if you absolutely hate sports.

For years, I've made accurate sports predictions on television, radio, and newspaper articles, without the faintest idea of how the games are played or who is playing them. And believe me, I don't want to know. Whether you pride yourself with extensive knowledge of the teams, individual players, or sports themselves, or if you know from nothing like I do, it will in no way help or hinder your ability to make accurate predictions.

One morning I made an appearance on a popular radio morning show and was asked to make a predic-

tion about an upcoming Houston Oilers/Pittsburgh
Steelers game. I had been a frequent guest on the
program specifically to make predictions about upcoming sporting events, and it was common knowledge at the station that I knew absolutely nothing
about sports, but had the channeling ability to successfully predict the outcome of various games.

The same morning the producer of the show had
also invited a well-known Houston radio and television sports announcer to appear with me to give his
prediction about the game.

I channeled at the station, and my Angels told me
that the Pittsburgh Steelers were going to win the
game. I announced this over the radio, which did
not endear me to the Houston audience. The sports
announcer, who knew everything there was to know
about football, predicted the Houston Oilers were not
only going to win, but they were going to soundly
defeat Pittsburgh in a stunning upset, and the Steelers
would return home in disgrace. All the other sports
experts the station interviewed during the show that
morning agreed that Houston was going to win, and
I did become a little anxious, having given my un-
popular prediction to hundreds of thousands of listen-
ers, but my Angels remained firm. The Steelers were
going to win.

After I announced my prediction on the radio, I
was personally criticized, attacked, and teased for the
stand I took against the Oilers. Not a sports fan, I
really couldn't understand what all the big fuss was
about, but I went along with all the teasing and
played a good sport, remaining true to what my
Angels told me, even though all the experts were
firmly convinced I was completely crazy. Was I
scared I was wrong? You bet I was!

Although I felt confident I had channeled correctly, and my Angels remained certain about the outcome of the game, it still made me squirm to know that if I was wrong, I would be embarrassed in front of the station's whole audience. In addition, the sports announcer, who also hosted his own television show, was already promising me that he would never let me forget such a blunder and he would hold my psychic ability up to ridicule until the next millennium. Ultimately, I was most concerned that the radio audience would lose faith in the process of channeling.

It turned out to be a wonderful learning experience for everyone concerned. For you sports fans who care about this sort of thing, you may remember that the final score of the game played September 6, 1992, was Pittsburgh Steelers 29, Houston Oilers 24.

Predicting the Gender of a Baby

This has always been one my favorite ways of practicing my channeling ability. Pregnant women offer a wonderful opportunity for you to work on your intuitive skills, but unlike predicting sporting events, you'll have to wait for some time to check the accuracy of your prediction!

Simply write down the name of the mother and father, and the expected due date for the baby. Quite often, the time of the baby's arrival that I pick up from my Angels is different from the expected due date as determined by the physician, so I also record my due date information, along with the baby's gender, to check later for accuracy.

If you don't know any pregnant women, use television or magazines as a good source of information about pregnancies. If the expectant mother is a celebrity, you can rest assured that the birth will be announced publicly and you'll be able to confirm your Angelic information.

Additional, more in-depth information you'd be able to access from your Angels besides gender and due date of baby, would be weight and height of baby, coloring of baby, any difficulties for the mother or baby during the birthing process, if the pregnancy involves a single or multiple birth, and the health of the infant and new mother.

Several years ago, the husband of a friend came to my office for a private session. He and his wife had a wonderful marriage and four beautiful little daughters.

During his reading, one of his Angels told him of the certainty of another impending pregnancy. He was extremely surprised and commented something to the effect that, "Oh no! We're definitely *not* trying for another baby! We already have four children! You must have your signals crossed!"

His Angels went on to describe the little boy that was coming to them, when his wife would conceive, and what the baby's due date would be. He left my office quite convinced that his Angels were somehow wrong or that I had misinterpreted the intuitive information.

A short time later, his wife called to tell me about her unexpected pregnancy and that through prenatal testing, they had discovered it was a boy!

This story illustrates that in addition to an *existing* pregnancy, you may very well receive intuitive information about an *impending* conception and pregnancy long before the expectant mother and father!

Predicting Current Events

Current events provide a wealth of opportunities to build your channeling ability.

You may predict political elections by writing down the names of the candidates, the date, and location where the election will be held.

You may predict the outcome of a military invasion by writing down the names of the warring factions and the location of the confrontation.

You may predict the future economic climate for any country in the world, the rise and fall of national or international stock markets, the stability of interest rates, and the financial future for industries that effect your abundance and financial security. To practice receiving information on any financial topic, you must write down the financial question, along with the day's date, and simply ask for Angelic information. Even if your channeled information may seem nonsensical or unexpected to you at the time, be certain to take detailed notes that you can confirm as the dynamics from your reading begin to unfold.

You may predict weather patterns such as tropical storms, hurricanes, and the possibilities of earthquakes, tornadoes, and other natural disasters. Although you may be reluctant to seek such negative information, it is reassuring to discover that no such storms are coming to your area. If a serious storm is expected, you'll have plenty of warning and will have the time to take necessary precautions.

Another very positive element in channeling weather patterns is that you'll easily be able to confirm your channeled information, as it is certain to appear on television and in newspapers. You'll be surprised at how much information you'll be able to receive and how you can build your confidence by accessing Angelic information about mother nature.

To ask about upcoming weather patterns, write down your specific question including the location you're asking about, the day's date, and you'll receive the information.

Practicing with Photographs

This exercise is always a favorite at my channeling seminars. Without exception the audience is always shocked at how much accurate Angelic information they can receive by looking at a photograph of a stranger. It is important for the photograph to include a subject that is looking directly into the camera, so as to allow the reader to get into the "energy" of the person. The photographs may include individuals who are living or deceased, and the same intuitive information may also be received when looking at a photograph of an animal!

This is such a fun exercise and one that really helps build an incredible amount of confidence. I recommend you invite several friends to your home for an evening of channeling. Ask them to bring photographs of family or loved ones for the rest of the group to use to build their channeling skills. Each participant is to choose the photograph(s) they would most like to "read," and one by one, each member of the group is to describe, in as much psychic detail as possible, the person in the photograph.

In this verbal exercise it is unnecessary to write anything down in order to receive Angelic information. The photograph of the subject provides the same kind of intuitive input for your Angels as does the writing of his or her name.

Practicing with Psychometry

Psychometry is the ability to channel by holding an object, usually something that belongs to another person, about whom you wish to receive intuitive information.

This is another excellent exercise conducted in a group setting. Ask the participants to bring with them material objects that belong(ed) to another person, for other members of the group to "read" from. Each participant is to choose the object that appeals to them most, and after holding the object and concentrating, the group member is to describe the person who owned the object. The participant may also receive a wealth of additional information, including physical health, emotional well-being, and state of mind of the object's owner. This is another wonderful exercise to work on at the same time your assembled group is practicing with the photographs. This exercise also helps build impressive confidence in the participant's channeling ability.

This is a verbal exercise, and therefore, it is unnecessary to write anything down to receive intuitive information. The material object itself will yield significant and detailed information to you and your Angels because it is saturated with the energy of its owner.

Practicing by Channeling for Others

This is an excellent exercise technique if you are having difficulty really believing that you are receiving Angelic communication, and what you have been "picking up" intuitively for yourself isn't just coming from inside your own head.

If you do a reading for someone else, and you receive intuitive information for them about things you couldn't have possibly known, you'll become convinced very quickly that you are truly channeling. It will be extremely reassuring and a great help in building confidence in your own channeling ability to provide a friend or family member with necessary and important messages from their Angels.

Because it takes a lot of courage to practice your skills by channeling for someone else, I strongly recommend that you start building your confidence with the other practice techniques before you attempt an intuitive "reading."

If you practice, will you eventually have the ability and confidence to channel for someone else and receive accurate information? Of course you will!

There will be two distinct objectives when you provide channeled information to someone else. First, you will be providing them with Angelic information that confirms what they already know. This is not at all surprising. It is to be expected. After all, their Angels have been regularly communicating with them and are probably trying to provide the very same information that they've just given you to repeat.

For example, you may be doing a reading for your best friend, Martha. You receive information from her Angels that she is about to be promoted at work. She indicates that she already suspected that. Or perhaps you receive the information that she is supposed to start her own business. Martha replies that starting a business was something she had been thinking about for a long time. Although she was already expecting a promotion, and had the realization that she should start her own business, your Angelic confirmation of her prior awareness is very important for her to realize that her own instincts were correct and this will help her build confidence in her own intuitiveness.

Secondly, you will be providing Angelic information about dynamics that are going on behind the scenes that Martha had no clue was occurring.

For example, Martha asks you for Angelic information about her husband, Harvey. You receive the alarming information that Harvey has been conducting a long-standing love affair with his secretary, Myrna, who is about to become pregnant with his child. Or, perhaps you receive information that Martha has a tiny lump of cancer in her left breast, and by having an immediate surgical lumpectomy, she will have the opportunity to keep her breast, completely stop the growth of the cancer, and have many more years of good health.

Although unexpected, this information is incredibly valuable, because if Martha has a new awareness of something that is currently happening or just about to happen, she will either be able to prevent it altogether, or avoid the uncomfortable and sometimes traumatic experience of having an emotional rug pulled out from under her. Martha may not like what is occurring, but through your channeled information, you have diffused the stunning surprise element that could have taken her on an emotional roller-coaster ride of hideous proportions.

Several years ago I did a reading for a Houston client who was concerned that something "strange" was going on with her husband, who was living in New Zealand at the time.

My client stated they had a good relationship over the course of many years, and had mutually decided

to temporarily endure such a vast distance between
them in order for the husband to start a new business.
Their plan was for her to join him a short time later,
when money permitted.

She said her husband sounded "funny" on the
telephone during their last conversation and she was
worried. She had asked him if anything was wrong
and he reassured her that things were just fine, that he
simply had been suffering from an unusual amount
of stress and pressure getting the new business off
the ground.

My client asked about the "funny" tone in her
husband's voice. Was it his health? Was he not feeling well? Had he lost all of their investment capital?
Did he change his mind about the business? Was he
just lonesome? She knew something was up, but felt
he hadn't told her exactly what the problem was so
as not to needlessly worry her.

During her session, we received the information
that something was definitely up. Her husband had
begun a love affair with a young woman he met
through his business and had fallen for her like a ton
of bricks.

My client was shocked. *This* she didn't expect. She
couldn't believe it at first. Then she asked for more
comprehensive information. I described the "other
woman," explained how they met, and where they
were meeting for their romantic trysts. This was yet
another unpleasant surprise. The lovers were meeting
in the home the husband had purchased for he and
my client to live in once she arrived in New Zealand!

Then pieces of the puzzle started to come together
for my client. She thought she heard a woman's
voice in the background when she talked with her
husband the previous week, but when she asked him

about it, he laughed and told her she was crazy. She had also been wondering why the telephone answering machine was always on at home, even when he was supposed to be there. Her husband had also stopped being as romantic as he usually was before he left Houston and "now that she thought about it" was being uncharacteristically cold and indifferent to her. He had also stopped discussing her impending arrival in New Zealand with the same enthusiasm and eagerness as he had in prior conversations.

After all the pieces started to fall neatly in place, she knew in her heart that her Angels were right. Her husband was having an affair with another woman.

Her next question to me was, "Now what should I do? I want to hear it from his own lips! I want proof that he has betrayed me! I can just picture the two of them! And in what was to be my own home!"

If she had to have proof, her Angels told her, then she should directly confront him. She should tell him that a psychic "saw" the girlfriend with him and that they were frequently meeting in his home for their romantic encounters. She also needed to physically describe the girlfriend and relay how long the affair had been going on.

My client expressed great hesitation about laying all her intuitive cards on the table, rather than hiring a private investigator to shoot compromising photographs of the couple. *Pictures* he could never refute.

Her Angels told her she didn't need to go to the expense of hiring an investigator. To get her proof, all she needed to do was follow through with the plan of action they just recommended. It would cost her nothing more than a long-distance telephone call. Her Angels also advised her to tape the conversation because her husband had already proved himself to be deceitful and would probably lie about the conversation ever having taking place, once he made his confession.

She tearfully left my office with a great deal of uncertainty about how she ought to proceed, but promised to call me with the results of whatever she had decided to do.

I heard from her several days later. She said she was absolutely heartbroken, but triumphant because she had her proof. With tape running, she called her husband and their conversation went like this:

SHE: "You know, honey, when we talked the other day, I was worried about something being wrong."

HE: "You're being too sensitive. I told you everything is fine!"

SHE: (Tearfully) "I'm afraid you're having an affair."

HE: "An affair! How could you think that? Don't you trust me?"

SHE: "Yes, but everything seems to add up to that—"

HE: "You're crazy! Why would I want to ruin what we have together? I know you'd leave me if I so much as looked at another woman!"

SHE: (Silence)

HE: "Honey?"

SHE: "I'm here."

HE: "I love you."

SHE: (Silence)

HE: "I can't believe you'd accuse me! Another woman? And I've been doing nothing but fixing our house up just for you—"

SHE: "Oh, really? Is that what you're doing there at night? Picking color schemes?"

HE: (Enraged) "Will you stop cross-examining me? I can't believe this! You've gone off the deep end! You have no proof—"

SHE: (Sniffling) "Actually, I do. And here it is. I know you hired your girlfriend originally as a customer service rep. She is twenty-six, about five-six, and very slender. She has dark hair and blue eyes. She is almost divorced from her second husband. You've been seeing her for exactly two months. The two of you drive separate cars, hers is a Volvo, and you meet at our house, approximately three times a week. She is beginning to get upset that you never take her out in public, that the two of you always eat in. After these dinner 'dates,' she spends the night with you. That's why the machine is always on when I call. You lie to her and say you're going to get a divorce as soon as I move to New Zealand, which you really have no intention of doing. Want any more proof than that?"

HE: "Oh my God, I can't believe you found out! You're in Houston and I'm in frigging New Zealand! What did you do? Hire a private investigator?"

SHE: "No. A psychic!"

When you consider practicing your channeling skills by doing an intuitive reading for someone else, I strongly urge you, I beg you, to only consider doing readings for people who are open and enthusiastic about the intuitive process.

If you attempt to read for someone who doesn't

really want intuitive information, or who is closed, negative, disbelieving, or ridiculing of the process of channeling, then you are planning to fail. You'll make an exciting, enjoyable process frustrating and depressing, and I want to caution you that if you read for people like that, you'll truly make yourself drained, miserable, and you'll feel the hard-earned confidence in your channeling ability disappearing. Look for people who are open, enlightened, curious, enthusiastic, and positive about your new ability and your need to practice.

One of my clients, a successful entrepreneur, is always a joy to read for because of his intuitive awareness, openness, and enlightenment. His faith in his own intuitiveness has allowed him to create and maintain a number of lucrative businesses in diverse industries.

However, as open as he was, when I told him about an unexpected, upcoming business opportunity in the entertainment industry, he laughed and expressed great disbelief. His Angels told him to prepare for a small movie role in a film starring Charlie Sheen!

The next time I saw him for a private session, about four months later, he had already completed his role in the film and was enthusiastically looking forward to pursuing other film roles.

Although initially it seemed incredibly unlikely (to both me and my client) that he would have the opportunity to work as a film actor, he remained open to listening to the intuitive information as provided by his Angels.

Once you have chosen a (wonderfully enlightened) subject to channel for, ask them to prepare questions to ask of their Angels before the session, so you have a meaningful agenda and will use your time together most productively. Your subject's questions should represent their greatest priorities. Set a time limit for the session so as not to completely drain your batteries, and I suggest you tape the channeling session so there is an exact record of all the Angelic information you have worked so hard to receive. The tape will also help provide positive feedback of your accuracy. To begin, I suggest you write your subject's name and age on a sheet of paper, along with the day's date. Take a deep breath, concentrate, call in their Angels, and you're off and running!

Practicing at a Psychic Fair

Developing your channeling ability by participating in a psychic fair is by far the most challenging of all the practice techniques and one that you should consider only after you have already felt some success in reading for friends and family members.

Even after you have built a strong level of confidence in prior readings for friends and family, I want to make you aware that channeling for a complete stranger is a totally different experience, but one that you'll be fully capable of with a little practice.

There are great advantages of taking this kind of risk. A psychic fair is a spectacular training ground for you to develop your ability to receive Angelic information quickly, because you will only have ten or fifteen minutes with each subject. Psychic fairs generally attract people who have a multitude of questions, ranging from their health, to their life's work, to the state of their relationships, to the well-being of their children.

Although at the time I was absolutely scared to death, I found the experience of participating in several psychic fairs invaluable when I was first working with my Angels to develop my ability. I recall being asked questions that shocked and surprised me, that interestingly enough, in all my years of experience, I have never been asked since!

One Saturday, at my very first psychic fair, a middle-aged woman sat at my small table with an obviously reluctant man in tow, who she explained was her second husband. He was the stepfather to her two young, beautiful teenaged daughters. The woman proceeded to tell me in a hissing whisper that the girls had moved out of the family home because they had both accused their stepfather of sexually molesting them! With tears in her eyes, she angrily gestured toward her husband and confrontationally demanded that I channel to determine the truth. Should she believe her daughters' account of being victimized, or her husband's steadfast denial of their allegations? Wide-eyed, I stared at the husband, who sat strangely passive and emotionless, regarding me more with curiosity than any fear of discovery.

At the moment our eyes locked, however, the husband abruptly jumped out of his chair and bolted to the bathroom. Luckily for me, I had a small window of opportunity to speak with the woman alone. My heart was pounding furiously, but I was able to receive the Angelic information the woman needed so badly to confirm her own suspicions, and I slowly and calmly passed it along to her. Her husband did indeed molest the two girls.

Not all of the questions you receive will be of such a serious nature, but if you decide to take the plunge and work a psychic fair, a good rule of thumb is to expect the unexpected, and like the Boy Scouts, be prepared for anything.

If you are strongly considering becoming a professional psychic channel, then regularly participating in psychic fairs is a must for you to make an intelligent decision about how fulfilled you feel accessing Angelic information for others, and if you really like the process of passing it along. A psychic fair will also help establish an awareness of who you are and how you work, and is an excellent source of networking within the community.

The method of preparation is exactly the same with any channeled session. It makes no difference if the subject is your Aunt Vera, who is seated at your kitchen table, or a stranger who wants a reading from you at a psychic fair. Write your subject's name and age on a sheet of paper, take a deep breath, concentrate, and call in their Angels.

Psychic Etiquette:
The Do's and Don't's of Providing
Channeled Information to Others

Once you have opened your channeling ability, and are regularly communicating with your Angels, an amazing phenomenon takes place. A visible band of electrical light begins to radiate from you and is perceptible to all the guardian Angels on the other plane.

Once your electrical energy becomes visible, any number of guardian Angels will be attracted to you, because you are open to receiving their information and responding to them in a two-way communication.

Why would other people's guardian Angels spend

their precious time and energy communicating with you? To encourage you to pass their messages on to those whom they guide, as if you're delivering a psychic "telegram."

Because many people remain unaware of their ability to channel, it becomes a very frustrating, tedious process for their Angels to productively communicate with them. Now that you are so fluently channeling, their Angels consider you "the next best thing to being there."

I always try to speak with people after they have attended my channeling seminars to ask what they are experiencing and how they are coming along with their Angelic communication. A majority of the people I've spoken to comment that they have been visited by a number of guardian Angels who request they pass along a variety of information to friends, family members, business colleagues, acquaintances, and even strangers. This is such a common occurrence that I want you to expect that it will happen to you and be fully aware and prepared for the experience.

Although they will have different personalities, communicating with guardian Angels other than your own will involve exactly the same communication skills. They will speak to you with gentle persuasion in the hopes that you will be kind enough to pass along intuitive information that they can't seem to communicate, because their "guidee" is too closed, too distracted, too unaware, or too emotionally upset. Other people's Angels may contact you once in a lifetime, or they may consistently come to you with requests to pass along information. The more willing you are to deliver their "telegrams," the more often they will ask you to do so.

Whether or not you decide to pass Angelic information to another person is completely your decision. I promise you won't be accruing any negative karmic brownie points if you refuse. The Angels will simply search for another person who is productively channeling.

If you do decide to pass along intuitive information, you don't necessarily have to say "Mary, your guardian Angel just told me to tell you that if you're late one more day this week, your boss is going to fire you!"

Unless she was very enlightened, Mary would probably think that you'd gone off the deep end. Instead, you may want to preempt your statement with, "Mary, I have this intuitive feeling that . . ." You'd still be passing along the very same Angelic information, but you wouldn't be startling or shocking Mary, or worse, causing unintentional amusement.

When I first started channeling, there were so many other guardian Angels who visited and asked me to pass along "telegrams" to other people, I was really astonished! I believed that if they came to me and asked so nicely, I was the girl to do the job. Who was I to say no to them? Was I wrong! I learned the hard way that I was not required to deliver the psychic telegrams, but that it was completely my personal decision, and I was to use my discretion each and every time I was asked.

How did I learn the hard way? By eagerly and enthusiastically passing intuitive information to other people without concern for their feelings, like someone who had just gotten a spiffy new camera and wants to take everyone's picture, whether they are willing to be in the photograph or not.

For example, every time I would meet a new man and go out on a date, his Angel would visit and ask me to provide information. The conversation with my date would go like this: "Tom, your guardian Angel told me last night to tell you that you need a check-up. You have a heart murmur that could cause some problems later in life . . ." I would scare the daylights out of Tom, we'd have a very early evening, and of course he would never call me again.

I was also regularly asked to pass intuitive information to strangers. It happened frequently when I was doing errands in grocery stores, dry cleaners, shoe repair shops, banks, and department stores. I would receive Angelic information loud and clear for someone standing next to me.

Once, I was in the grocery store after work and a woman came and stood next to me in frozen foods, perusing the ice cream section. I received a "telegram" for her.

"Excuse me," I said, eagerly approaching her and full of helpful enthusiasm. "Those figures you included in the report that you just left on your boss's desk? They're all wrong. You were in too much of a hurry to proof as well as you normally do because of your date tonight. You better go back to the office and do it over. It could be the difference between a raise and losing your job. Your blind date is going to cancel, anyway."

The woman remained silent, her eyes as big as saucers. She backed away from me in utter disbelief and wheeled her cart in the opposite direction as quickly as if she had just had an encounter with someone carrying the bubonic plague.

Why was that happening, I wondered? I was

passing along Angelic information! Her Angels asked me to pass it along! Why was I so uncomfortable? Why did I feel so embarrassed? I would never intentionally try to make anyone self-conscious or frightened.

It took some time for me to realize that it was a matter of privacy. No one likes their privacy violated and that was what I was doing by approaching them with unrequested Angelic information. It didn't matter how good my intentions were or that the information was coming directly from their Angels. I was violating their privacy.

Because it was such a hard learning experience for me, and I encountered so many negative responses to delivering my "telegrams," I remain ultrasensitive to other people's feelings and their right to privacy.

In spite of my philosophy, I still sometimes pass along unrequested Angelic information. My rule of thumb is this: I pass along intuitive information if it involves either a person's health or physical safety. I make only those two exceptions.

Why do I make any exceptions? If I had been given prior information about someone's health that could have made a difference in their longevity and I neglected to pass it along, I know I wouldn't be able to live with the knowledge that perhaps I could have made a difference.

If I had been given information about someone's safety that could have ultimately prevented a sexual assault, an abduction, or a murder, and I neglected to pass it along and then heard about the tragedy taking place, I would never be able to rationalize my silence.

So even if I have to approach a stranger with intuitive information about their health of safety, I do so knowing full well what their response will most likely be. But by following this rule of thumb, I have had the opportunity to pass along unrequested Angelic information that has saved three lives.

How to Choose a Good Psychic Channel

Although I have written this book to teach you how to directly and skillfully communicate with your individual guardian Angels, on occasion, you will want or need another person to channel for you no matter how well you develop your own intuitive skills.

Perhaps you simply want objective confirmation of information you have already channeled, or perhaps you are working through extremely difficult issues and need to make certain that you aren't misinterpreting or misunderstanding the intuitive information provided by your Angels.

When I want sensitive information confirmed, or when I want the luxury of someone else accessing Angelic information for me, I call my mother, who is also a very accomplished channel.

If you decide to seek out a professional, you will need to consider the following insider's criteria of how to chose a knowledgeable, reputable psychic channel. My guidelines are as follows:

1. Rather than searching through the telephone directory, find a professional channel through a referral from someone you know and respect. If you share a similar outlook or philosophies with a friend, family member, or co-worker, chances are you'll

be satisfied with a referral from them, whether it's for a physician, attorney, hairdresser, accountant, or psychic channel. If no one you know has visited with a channel, or they've had a bad experience, or in the event you don't want to discuss your visit to a psychic channel with anyone, call a metaphysical clinic, school, or bookstore for a recommendation. They should be very knowledgeable about good people in your area.

2. When a physic channel is recommended, be sure that when you call to make your appointment, you inquire as to how long that person has been in business. It is my very strong philosophy that if you're going to the trouble and expense to visit a psychic channel, you'll want to have a session with someone who is more experienced than you are and who has developed their channeling ability to a greater extent than you have. Or why go? You'd be wasting your precious time, money, and energy. If they're not as experienced as you are after practicing the techniques in this book, you need to be aware *before* you walk into their office so you're not disappointed.

3. Ask about the channel's fee structure. What exactly are the fees, and what will you get for your money? Are the sessions a fixed length? Can you ask as many questions as you like during that time? Are there any additional fees? If so, for what? Beware of the psychic who says, "Oh! You want that information? I can get it, but it will cost you an additional . . ."

The psychic must openly, professionally, and intelligently answer your questions about how they work. If the psychic responds to your questions in a vague, dismissive, or hostile way, you need to thank him for his time, hang up the telephone, and continue your search.

4. Before you make an appointment, you must also inquire if the kind of questions you may ask are unlimited. Will the channel allow and encourage you to ask the questions that are your current priorities? After all, getting answers to your questions is the reason you want to make the appointment in the first place! Are there certain topics the psychic can't access information about? Can they access very specific information? You don't want to visit someone who makes broad or general statements such as, "Oh, yes, you're going to get the new job, but I can't be sure if it will be in three weeks, or three months, or three years."

In my opinion, if you're going to visit a professional channel, you deserve much more explicit information than that. After reading this book and practicing, you'll be able to receive much more specific information yourself!

Also be certain to discuss your reason for making the appointment ahead of time, so you'll have confidence that the channel you are going to visit has the experience to comprehensively answer your particular questions.

5. Ask if the channel has equipment to tape your session, and if it is necessary for you to supply your own tape. If they do not offer that convenience, you must insist on bringing your own taping equipment with you, plus a new, high quality tape to record the session you have with them. If they refuse to allow you to tape the session, do not schedule an appointment.

A good channel will want you to have an exact record of the channeled information they provide to you. I insist on taping every session in my office, even if a client doesn't want the tape. After each session, I give my client the tape and they're free to do whatever they wish with it. The channeled information I've accessed belongs to them. They've given me an even exchange of energy for my time, and it's part of my responsibility to provide an exact record of what we've discussed.

Don't even consider trying to record the session by taking copious notes. Very often a channel speaks too quickly for you to get it all in writing, and you're bound to miss something. It's far too distracting and a waste of time for you to be forced to take dictation. Why should you have to go to all that work?

6. Pointedly ask if your session will remain confidential. Unless you're a celebrity, you probably won't have to be concerned about any of your channeled information ending up on the front page of a tabloid. But whatever you ask should remain very private and confidential, and should not leave the psychic's office.

Over the years, I've had sessions with clients who were very well known and therefore worried about my philosophies of confidentiality. I believe that a channel's code of ethics must reflect those of a psychiatrist, priest, or attorney. Personally, I wouldn't visit a psychic who frequents television talk shows to discuss famous people and her predictions for them.

How did I become so militant in my philosophy of privacy? I began my practice a number of years ago by naively complying with local Houston radio and television media to answer questions and make predictions about famous individuals who were not among my clientele. And although I was repeatedly pressured, I staunchly refused to publicly discuss the identity of any client or what he/she discussed with me in my office.

It occurred to me early on that if I wouldn't discuss the identity of any client of mine because it was a gross violation of their privacy and trust in me, why would I even consider discussing someone whom I'd never even met?

Without someone's prior approval, publicly making predictions about the condition of their health, their marriages, children, careers, and other facets of their lives is the worst kind of exploitation and makes me feel physically sick.

Now I always refuse the "opportunity" to appear on local or national television to discuss personal predictions for celebrities or anyone else, for that matter. I simply won't do it and I'll continue to turn down those interviews.

A word of caution if you are a celebrity or a well-known person: be very, very discriminating and selective about whom you chose to channel for you. You certainly don't want an exploitive psychic (or astrologer, Tarot card reader, etc.) coming forward at any time in the future to divulge intimate information about you to the media looking to ride on your wave of success.

7. During your session with a psychic, be aware of any obvious hostilities that seem to be coloring the channeled information they give you.

For example, a number of years before I became a channel, I visited a female psychic who had obvious unresolved issues involving men. During my session, when I would inquire about the possibilities of a special man coming into my life, she would become extremely aggravated and hostile because I would even ask such a question. She seemed excessively angry that I was so unenlightened as to even want or need a special man in my life.

"After all," she said, gesturing to an open window from which we could see a number of young men jogging down her street, "they're all alike. It doesn't matter which one you choose. Eventually, you'll be disappointed, miserable, and heartbroken just like all the rest of us."

Needless to say, the reading didn't go well. I didn't receive the most important information I needed because of her unresolved hostilities. Not only was my time, money, and energy totally wasted, but I was so drained and depressed when I left her home, that I bought a pound of chocolate and ate it all on the way back to my office!

8. Beware of the psychics who imply that only they can receive channeled information, or ones who try to scare you into believing that you can't or shouldn't make any decision without their psychic input. That behavior is very manipulative and controlling, and is probably based on extorting as much money from you as possible.

   If you've truly taken the time to practice, you already know that you can capably channel to access your own intuitive information from your Angels. No matter how good a channel these psychics may prove to be, run as fast as you can in the opposite direction. They are more interested in your wallet than your spiritual evolvement.

9. Don't allow a psychic (or anyone else, for that matter) to pressure you to make an appointment.

You'll know from your initial telephone conversation if that person is right for you

If you've already had a session with a channel you'll know if you want to schedule another appointment. When my clients ask if and when they should come back for another session with me, I tell them that they'll know intuitively when they need to return, and to call back at that time to make another appointment.

10. No matter how convincing a psychic might be, I want you to realize there is no such thing as a curse.

There Is No Quick Fix

I would like to expand on the "curse" issue. From the time I began working as a psychic channel, I have frequently been surprised at the number of thinking, intelligent men and women who have frantically called my office because they were convinced there had been a curse placed upon them.

How could they possibly believe they were "cursed"? Because they recently had a consultation with a psychic, usually one with a name like Madame Lagonga, who gave them a short reading for a very small fee, and was amazingly specific. She described their career, lifestyle, friends, and family members with stunning accuracy, and in doing so, gradually built a believable level of credibility.

They would report that after she completed her psychic disclosures about their personal and professional life, Madame Lagonga alarmingly "discovered" that a curse had been placed upon them by a disgruntled family member or vindictive business colleague who wished them harm. Madame Lagonga urgently warned that if they didn't get the curse removed with great dispatch, they would suffer dire consequences.

Rational, intelligent people can be cleverly manipulated by Madame Lagonga because she is so accurate about all the rest of their psychic information, so who are they to argue about a curse?

"What can I do about the curse?" the person would ask of her.

"Ahhh," she would reply, "it's your good fortune that you are here with me! I have years of experience removing curses of all kinds. I can see that your curse will be particularly difficult to remove. If I don't remove it, I "see" that you will lose your job [spouse, money, home, good health, etc.] and I will not be responsible."

Madame Lagonga would then vaguely detail how long it would take her to remove the curse with prayer and explained the secret procedure of filling a special sack with several personal effects from the "curse" victim, along with other items, including various kinds of animal by-products.

The "curse removal" ritual would be completed when Madame Lagonga took the bag of paraphernalia to an undisclosed location for burial, with the intention of resurrecting the items for inspection at some time in the future for her to determine if the curse had been lifted.

From my experience with what people have told me, the fee for the "curse removal" ritual normally starts at several thousand dollars and can climb quickly into the tens of thousands.

How could rational, intelligent people be bamboozled by such chicanery? You'd be surprised at how convincing these con artists can be. After all, they have years of experience making a living by hood-winking vulnerable customers.

I want to prevent you from becoming a victim by arming you with the truth. First of all, no matter what anyone tells you, there is no such thing as a curse.

It is impossible for another person, no matter how much they may dislike you, or how much psychic or intuitive ability they have, to place a curse or spell on you. Don't ever be fooled into believing that your life is controlled by anything or anyone other than you.

No outside influence can make you lose your job, your significant other, or your good health. If you are not currently happy, or successful, or satisfied with your life, it has nothing whatsoever to do with any outside influence holding you back and making it impossible for you to move ahead. Your success, peace of mind, and feelings of happiness come only from what you create for yourself on a daily basis.

In addition, don't expect any quick, easy solutions to difficult situations with the purchase of metaphysical supplies created "just for you" by a con artist eager to prey upon your innocence, trust, or vulnerability. Never invest your hard-earned money in magic potions, blessed rice, special candles, charms with mysterious powers, animal by-products, "curse removers," or any other expensive but totally senseless paraphernalia.

Keep in mind that no potion or charm can possibly produce a pregnancy, force your boyfriend to return to you, open new job opportunities, create chaos in someone else's life, or help you win the lottery.

Please understand there is no quick fix for any problem, challenge, or hardship you encounter. All that you accomplish and achieve comes from developing faith in yourself, taking necessary risks, and doing quite a bit of hard work. There are no shortcuts.

CHAPTER TEN

Questions and Answers

The following questions have been asked over the years by participants attending my channeling seminars. I hope you find the answers insightful and informative in your quest to be more fully enlightened and develop the relationship with your Angels.

What happens when I feel a deceased family member around me all the time, and then suddenly, the feeling of their energy vanishes?

There are several reasons why you would no longer feel the energy of a deceased family member.

After a loved one passes to the other plane, he or she will frequently worry about our well-being and choose to hover protectively around us. At the time our deceased family member becomes assured that we no longer need their guidance or protection because we are functioning productively, he or she moves on to build a new existence in heaven.

In addition, we may no longer feel the presence

of a deceased loved one because he or she has returned to the physical plane in a new physical body for yet another lifetime. Once a soul enters another physical body and embarks on a new lifetime, we are no longer able to channel with that individual as a heavenly being because they are no longer on the other plane. However, if we wish to receive information about their new lives here on the physical plane, it is certainly available through our Angels.

Is channeling with a deceased loved one easier than communicating with a guardian Angel?

Channeling with deceased loved ones is very much like communicating with your Angels because they all exist side-by-side in heaven, or what I refer to as "the other plane." However, remember that you already have a familiarity with your deceased loved one, and that prior relationship will definitely make communicating with them easier and seemingly more tangible.

In my office, so many clients have begun their private sessions by describing the recent death of a loved one, and then breathlessly exclaim, "You might think I'm crazy, but I saw my Aunt Sara last night! Then this morning, she spoke to me in my car!"

I never realized until I began hosting my Angel seminars how many people had experienced the phenomenon of seeing and hearing deceased loved ones that have returned to speak with them. It is startlingly easy to communicate with Aunt Sara, because you can immediately recognize Aunt Sara. You remember the sound of her voice, the kind of language she used, and how she looked when she was still here on the physical plane. As incredible as it may seem, you know you actually spoke with Aunt Sara because she remains so familiar to you. With a little practice, you can become just as familiar with your guardian Angels.

Can we get intuitive information about another person without his or her permission?

Most definitely, and it is not considered an invasion of privacy to do so.

Our Angels believe that any question we ask about another person is valid and has merit as long as we seek the information to help us solve a problem, work on an issue, improve a relationship, or move forward spiritually.

In all my years of channeling, I have only been told once that intuitive information about another person was not available for my client.

The situation was quite amusing. My client asked about her brother's love life and whether he and his girlfriend would eventually marry. Her brother's Angels quickly appeared and pointedly demanded that I tell my client, "It is none of her business!"

Although I was very surprised to have received such a terse Angelic response because my client's question seemed caring and appropriate, I repeated what they said to her. She threw back her head, roared with laughter, and explained "That's what my brother always tells me!"

Normally, you'll have no problem accessing any information you desire about another person. My experience has been that Angels are forever chastising us for not asking enough questions of them!

If you're not sure what to ask, please refer to the

comprehensive list of questions found in Chapter Four.

Lately, I'm waking up in the middle of the night and I can't go back to sleep. Does this have anything to do with my Angels?

It is very likely that the reason you awaken in the middle of the night is because your Angels are trying to provide intuitive information to you at a time when you are least distracted, rather than risking confusion during a hectic and busy day. The next time you find your self wide awake in the middle of the night, you may not be suffering from insomnia at all. Most likely, one of your Angels is trying to speak with you.

When this occurs, you may want to either reschedule the "meeting" to a more convenient time, or take immediate advantage of the intuitive information your Angel is trying to provide to you by channeling using a notebook and pen you keep by the side of your bed.

Can Angelic information just pop in my head without my asking for it?

Absolutely, and far more frequently than you might imagine. This is the process of knowingness, which is the most common form of Angelic communication. Until you learn to speak with your Angels in a two-way conversation, they "pop" important intuitive information into your head that you probably perceive as part of your own thought processes or "gut instincts."

For example: One clear fall evening an inner voice (that you may feel as a "gut instinct") urges you to quickly drive your brand-new car to safety inside the garage. Although it makes no logical sense to you at the time, you decide to trust your instincts. Shortly thereafter, the sky darkens ominously and without warning an unexpected hailstorm causes widespread damage to motor vehicles in your neighborhood.

Why do so many people choose to return to the physical plane now when there is so much violence in the world?

There has always been a great deal of ignorance, danger, and violence on the physical plane. Each period of history speaks volumes about what people have had to endure and the suffering they have had to encounter.

In a previous lifetime, you may have lived through the terror of the bubonic plague, been tortured as an innocent victim of the Spanish Inquisition, starved through the Irish potato famine, drowned as a passenger of the ill-fated *Titanic,* or committed suicide because you lost a hard-earned fortune in the Great Depression.

Why would someone deliberately choose to return to such difficulties and hardships when they could remain in heaven?

When we live on the spiritual plane as heavenly beings, we consider it a great opportunity to come back in a physical body to continue working on our issues and accomplishing a life's work in which we make a difference in the quality of other people's lives.

The physical plane with all of its hardships represents a training ground, or a spiritual boot camp, where we have the continual opportunity to rise to the occasion and improve our level of enlightenment by the way we conduct ourselves and through the kindness, respect, and consideration we show other people.

What is "white light?"

White light is a beam of heavenly electrical energy that invisibly radiates around our physical bodies to protect and to heal.

Quite often, you'll hear someone suggest that you "surround yourself with white light," to manifest a greater abundance of the protective and healing properties of the electrical energy.

How do you surround yourself with white light? Close your eyes and envision the entire length of your body enveloped in silvery white energy.

Many people have asked my feelings about how protective white light really is. I have met individuals who feel that they are completely safe from any kind of harm after they have gone through the exercise of increasing the white light surrounding them.

I do not agree. I fully believe in the existence of white heavenly light because I can always feel it radiating around my body, and I have psychically "seen" it radiating from clients during their private sessions. However, because of what I have experienced with violent crime while working with private investigators and families of crime victims, I am much more of a believer in continually using my intuitiveness to avoid harm or injury. I do not believe that relying on white light alone provides sufficient protection against unexpected mishaps, injury, or illness.

Does your body have any physical reactions while you are channeling?

Yes, it mostly certainly does! I am normally cold all the time, but as soon as I start to channel, my body temperature rises and I feel as if I am experiencing hot flashes.

In addition, when Angels provide me with particularly important or significant information to give to a client, my eyes fill slightly with tears, and it is quite common for me to get "goosebumps."

Many of my clients gasp and rub their arms because they too feel such an overwhelming goosebump sensation. This is Angelic confirmation about the channeled information provided during our private sessions together.

If I begin to channel when I have a mild headache, it vanishes very quickly because of the increase in the electrical energy that flows through my body. I also lose any sense of time when I channel, as well as the physical sensations of pain, hunger, or thirst.

Although many hours of channeling can be draining, the process fills me with a spiritual and emotional euphoric feeling that dramatically adds to my level of physical energy.

Why are some people born physically or mentally challenged?

Although it takes quite a bit of strength and courage, we all choose to experience mental and physical challenges in particular lifetimes to help us work through issues faster and more productively. Even if the mental or physical challenge is a slight one, it will obviously add to life's hardships, creating additional opportunities for spiritual growth.

Helen Keller is a wonderful example of someone who faced significant physical disabilities as a young child and worked to overcome them and live a life full of achievement and accomplishment.

Joseph Merrick, known as the "Elephant Man," faced horrific hardships because of his physical challenges. As a child he suffered through the cruelty and ridicule as an attraction in a carnival freak show and then grew into adulthood in a Victorian society that had little pity for the challenged or disabled.

The vitally important opportunity we have in lifetimes in which we face mental or physical challenges is that we learn firsthand about the issues of compassion, sensitivity, understanding, kindness, and being nonjudgmental through the difficulties and hardships we personally encounter. After personally experiencing a handicap or disability, we then carry the spiritual responsibility to treat others who endure such hardships with understanding, respect, kindness, and dignity. We are supposed to carry our heightened enlightenment into all future lifetimes with us as a beacon of light that we have to share with others who are less fortunate.

Do we choose how and when we are to die?

While we are still in heaven, we determine all the characteristics of our next life on the physical plane, including our gender, where we will live, who our parents will be, our economic background, the nature of our life's work, as well as the issues we intend to resolve.

We also decide how we will die and exactly when we will make the journey back to heaven. In some lifetimes it is when we are still small children. In others, we remain on the physical plane until we are quite elderly. Each lifetime is very special and unique.

Is every aspect of our lives fated and predetermined?

Absolutely not! All decisions we make on the physical plane involve free choice and free will. That is the reason we never know exactly how much we will ultimately accomplish in any lifetime until we return to heaven and take stock of what we have achieved.

Although we have the opportunity to make the decision of when and how we will die, our plans can be altered and we can die prematurely if we act carelessly. There are basically three problem areas that cause premature death on the physical plane.

For example, some individuals decide to commit suicide although they were not meant to die that way.

Some individuals are murdered because they refuse to listen to their Angels' warning about imminent danger.

Some individuals choose to neglect and abuse their physical bodies and create fatal illness where none were expected.

What happens if I start to grow spiritually through learning how to channel and my partner remains where he or she is now?

Frequently in my private sessions, when I'm asked about the underlying reason(s) why a couple is growing apart it is because one partner is moving forward with his or her enlightenment and the other partner remains stubbornly complacent.

Interestingly, once you begin to move forward and more fully develop your maturity, wisdom, and enlightenment, as well as begin to address and resolve issues, you build a momentum that fuels feelings of happiness, accomplishment, and achievement. So it is definitely not in your best interest to slow down or stop your progress, but instead, to try to inspire and encourage your partner to do the same.

Unfortunately, if your partner refuses to move forward and resolve issues, or to take more responsibility for his/her growth and spiritual evolvement, you will most likely find yourself growing out of the relationship and seeking a new partner who places a priority on their personal growth and expansion.

What happens when someone doesn't fulfill their purpose with another person?

You share a destiny, or purpose, with almost every person that comes into your life to fulfill a spiritual obligation or responsibility. The purpose you have with each person in your life was decided by the two of you in heaven before you were reborn into your present lifetime. It is of the utmost importance to your spiritual growth and evolution that you honor each and every commitment you have with other people.

The spiritual commitment may involve helping another person work through a trying emotional issue, mentoring them professionally, being a Mr./Ms. Wonderful, or perhaps helping him/her come into a better understanding of their gifts, talents, and abilities.

No matter what the purpose you have in his/her life, by accomplishing everything you are meant to with him or her, you are fulfilling your spiritual purpose and helping both of you again more enlightenment, happiness, and wisdom. To discover what your exact purpose is with the other people in your life, simply ask your Angels and you'll quickly receive the information.

When a person chooses (remember, you have the complete power to make daily choices about your behavior and decision making) not to fulfill their spiritual commitment to another person, the other person is forced into a scramble to find someone else with whom to accomplish the same spiritual task.

For example, a woman meets a man who is meant to be her Mr. Wonderful and with whom she is to marry and have a family. The relationship progresses to a certain point, until the man decides he is not up to the commitment of marriage and fatherhood. He discloses his decision not to honor his purpose with her and the couple breaks apart and forever loses the opportunity to emotionally interact and build a life together. The woman, who was happily ready and willing to fulfill her spiritual responsibility to him by being a wife and mother was let down by her significant other, who decided he could not honor his end of the spiritual commitment. The woman must then assume the heartbreaking burden of searching for another Mr. Wonderful with whom to accomplish the same spiritual tasks, which is an incredibly difficult position in which to find oneself spiritually.

What happens when someone commits suicide?

Upon the death of our physical bodies, we all proceed directly to heaven to begin new lives on the spiritual plane as heavenly beings.

However, when we commit suicide, we are kept

segregated from the general population for a certain period of time to heal.

When I have been asked to channel with deceased friends or family members who have committed suicide, I always "see" them suspended in a silvery-white cocoon filled with supercharged energy. While in the cocoon, they are not available to channel, but we may still receive information about them from Angels or other deceased friends or family members.

Interestingly when I have accessed past life information for a client who has attempted or is contemplating suicide, I often "see" that same person having committed suicide before in a past lifetime.

Our Angels become concerned that once we commit the very serious act of extinguishing our physical life, we may fall into the same pattern of behavior in future lifetimes when we become overwhelmed with depression, hardships, or difficulties.

For the victim of suicide, the cocoon of light is not meant as a punishment, but instead as an intense source of healing that is very soothing and recharging and counters the negative emotions of despair, hopelessness, and desperation experienced before the individual felt compelled to end his or her physical life.

It is such a gift to have the opportunity to return to the physical plane for each lifetime, and the window of time we have to accomplish our spiritual goals is so short, that committing suicide is considered one of the biggest no-no's in the universe.

Committing suicide immediately cuts short the already miniscule amount of time we have to get our spiritual agenda fully accomplished. Although we are never punished or penalized in heaven for our actions on the physical plane, we unknowingly add to our spiritual to-do list, creating even more difficulties for our next physical lifetime.

What happens when someone commits suicide if they are terminally ill?

If someone is terminally ill and they decide to end their physical life, they return to heaven like everyone else, but spend far less time in the healing cocoon than other victims of suicide before moving on with their spiritual life.

If I ask my Angels to appear to me will they do it?

Yes, there is a very good possibility that they will. All you have to do is request that they more tangibly appear before you.

From personal experience, I strongly recommend that you fully prepare yourself before you even make that request! Ask them to appear either at your side or directly in front of you so that you don't become startled or fearful.

I've had so many people express eagerness and enthusiasm to see their Angels tangibly that this question is one of the most popular in my channeling seminars.

Be advised that if you ask them to tangibly appear, they will very likely honor your request. I've received numerous telephone calls from astonished clients who exclaimed, "But I didn't think they'd really appear!" or "I was so scared I almost fainted!" or "I didn't believe they would really do what I asked!"

Remember, your Angels work for you behind the scenes to help you achieve everything possible while on the physical plane. If you make a reasonable request, they will make every attempt to rise above and beyond the call of duty to fulfill it.

Why do deceased friends or family members appear to some people and not to others?

Deceased friends or family members may spend time with all of their loved ones, but only certain people will have the level of intuitive sensitivity to pick up on their heavenly energy.

The more emotionally blocked, analytical, or disbelieving someone is, the less likely they will be to receive intuitive information from their Angels or any other heavenly being.

The greater your channeling ability and the more enhanced your intuitiveness, the easier it will be for you to "feel" your deceased loved one and continue to communicate with them.

Is it possible to ask Angels for proof of their existence?

As you are learning to channel, you may experience a feeling of doubt or uncertainty about whether your Angels really exist and if you can truly communicate with them.

At that point, you may decide you want tangible proof of their existence so you know that you aren't just imagining or fabricating the relationship you are developing with your Angels.

It is certainly possible to ask your Angels for a sign that they are working with you to help build trust in the relationship. It is important for you to make any and all requests of them that you believe will help speed or enhance your ability to channel productively.

You may ask for a tangible sign from them, but understand that it will be your Angels who decide exactly what the sign will be.

As proof of your Angels' existence, don't waste your time asking them to allow you to win the lottery, get pregnant, or meet your significant other. If those things are meant to happen for you they will, but not necessarily at your immediate request. They will happen, however, when you are most ready for them to occur.

Your Angels will decide upon a sign to prove their existence, and make no mistake, it will be tangible!

For example, they may appear before you as if they have a physical body. They may move material objects in your home or office. You may hear their voices speaking with you. A friend or relative with whom you haven't spoken in some time may call you with what you know is channeled information from your Angels. You could be headed directly for a car accident and your Angels suddenly remove you from harm's way. Or you may have locked your keys in the car like I did, and they may turn off your alarm, unlock the doors, and turn on the heat for you!

There are so many ways in which your Angels will continue to offer you proof of their existence. I have learned that the greatest proof for me has come from developing my ability to communicate with them and being showered with ongoing Angelic attention and affection. I've learned to listen to their suggestions about how I can consistently improve the quality of my life, and when I follow what they advise, I am always astonished at how much easier and more fulfilling my life can be.

Why do I feel the presence of my Angels at some times and not at other times?

We may feel a distance with one or more of our Angels at certain times because they have chosen to work behind the scenes to help facilitate greater opportunities for us.

When certain Angels decide they need to spend time away from us for any reason, I have generally found that they will communicate their absence to us, so we have a full understanding of where they are and exactly what they are doing on our behalf.

In addition, while you are building your sensitivity to your Angels, you may not feel their presence as consistently as you will when you have more fully developed your channeling ability.

If you begin to feel deserted, simply ask your Angels to talk with you and confirm that they are still there with you. Although one or more of your Angels may be working behind the scenes, rest assured that other Angels will have taken their place to work with you one-on-one.

Do I have to protect myself while channeling?

There is no reason to be concerned that you will attract an evil or mischievous entity to you when you begin to develop your channeling ability. No matter what you've heard, there are no flawed, evil spirits lying in wait in the hopes of manipulating you into heartbreak, misery, or ruin.

Only heavenly beings of the highest level of spiritual enlightenment are sanctioned by the universe to work as guardian Angels. These heavenly beings are the only spirits who will speak with you when you ask for information during the process of channeling.

Your individual guardian Angels have been very carefully selected for you to provide intuitive information of the highest caliber. You'll be able to fully depend on them to assist you in resolving issues, becoming successful in your life's work, and helping you create the best possible quality of life for you and your family.

What happens when we die? What does it mean when a person is dying and they have a vision of someone else who has died years before?

When our physical body expires, our soul makes the journey back to heaven.

If a person is experiencing the final stages of physical death and is finding it difficult to let go of their earthly body, or if he is tremendously fearful of what he will encounter when he dies, it can be very reassuring for a deceased friend or family member who has already made the journey to appear and provide encouragement.

All of us have what I refer to as a "welcoming committee" whose sole purpose is to help us release our physical bodies and support us on the journey back to the spiritual plane.

Many clients have shared stories about dying family members who suddenly begin to speak to someone who is visible only to them. The spirits with whom they are communicating are an assembly of heavenly beings who include their Angels, as well as deceased friends and family members who will accompany them on the journey to heaven and then provide assistance upon their return to help them get acclimated as quickly as possible to the spiritual plane.

Once the "welcoming committee" begins to appear, the person's physical death is imminent and the universe is providing the necessary support to make the journey as easy and effortless as possible.

The journey back to heaven is unique to each person but is most commonly made up of several stages.

First, your soul exits your physical body. Once your soul leaves your physical body, the body usually expires in seconds, minutes, or hours. In its departure, your soul may hover above your physical body for several moments while you communicate with your welcoming committee, and prepare for the journey back to heaven.

Next, it is very common to experience a tremendous rushing sensation as your soul, accompanied by your welcoming committee, speeds through a darkened, cylindrical tunnel toward a blinding white light. The white light is a representation of God and all the Angels in the universe.

Once your soul completes the journey through the tunnel, you are back in heaven and are once again a resident of the spiritual plane.

Upon your arrival in heaven, you are met by an expanded welcoming committee made up of additional friends and family members from past lifetimes who are waiting to happily welcome you to your new home.

Just as on the physical plane, in heaven you have the opportunity to establish a new life with the people you choose, performing the type of work you most enjoy.

What is a "walk-in?"

When we have the opportunity to return to the physical plane, we may do so in one of two vehicles.

Most often, the soul enters the body of a baby at birth or shortly thereafter.

The soul also has the opportunity to bypass the difficulties of childhood and directly enter an adult physical body that has been vacated by another soul.

A physical body can only accommodate one soul at a time. Why would a soul want to vacate its physical body? For the same reason that people decide to commit suicide. Life on the physical plane, with all of its problems, challenges, and hardships becomes far too overwhelming and they wish to live back in heaven.

When a person on the physical plane becomes so miserable with his life that he is no longer productive and is not expected to regain spiritual momentum at any time in the future, the universe begins to search for a soul in heaven that is desirous of making an exchange by returning to the physical plane.

Certain qualifications have to be met before a walk-in can occur.

The soul that currently inhabits the physical body must want to return to heaven very badly and long before the body was scheduled to expire. The person must make those feelings repeatedly known in the universe by manifesting with his or her Angels.

The incoming soul must commit to the difficult task of resolving or completing all of the other soul's ongoing issues that have already been initiated before it can move forward to achieve its own spiritual agenda.

Once another soul is found, the exchange takes place. The soul that inhabited the physical body returns to heaven in the same process as if the body naturally expired, and the incoming soul enters the physical body just as it would have entered the body of an infant.

How can you identify a walk-in?

An exchange of souls in an adult physical body is just as natural a process in the universe as a soul entering the body of an infant.

Once you become aware of the process, it will be easy for you to identify when an exchange of souls has first taken place.

The person who has experienced a soul exchange will suddenly appear to be a completely different person because he or she is!

The soul of the person you knew has gone to the spiritual plane and is gone forever from that physical body as if a death has taken place. The new soul that has taken resident in the physical body is a virtual stranger to you.

The depth and expression of the person's eyes will look totally different, as will their gestures, mode of dressing, patterns of speech, levels of emotional responsiveness, tastes, principles, sense of humor, and even the way they part their hair.

In essence, you'll be getting to know an entirely different person, even though they may inhabit a body that is very familiar to you.

What do you do if you discover a friend or family member has become a walk-in?

After you have made a determination that a walk-in has taken place, accept the fact that it occurred for the best benefit of both souls.

Obviously, your friend or family member felt he or she would be much happier on the spiritual plane.

Don't forget that now you have developed your ability to channel with heavenly beings, you'll easily be able to continue the communication with your departed loved one.

You'll know immediately if it is appropriate to begin a relationship with the new soul who has taken up residence by what your intuitiveness tells you.

If you remain uncertain, simply ask your Angels if you are meant to have a relationship with the new soul, and if you have any unresolved issues to complete with him or her.

How can I increase my sensitivity to the presence of my Angels?

There is an enjoyable exercise that I recommend in my channeling seminars to help increase your sensitivity to the presence of your Angels, and which can also dramatically increase your intuitive sensitivity to other people.

Call a small group of friends to meet in your home and advise them not to wear any type of perfume or cologne.

The first participant is to sit on a chair in the center of a room, and close his or her eyes.

It is best if the room is carpeted so the participant cannot recognize the sound of familiar footfalls. If the room you choose to use for this exercise is not carpeted, ask everyone to remove their shoes.

One by one, each person is to enter the room, and stand perfectly still approximately three feet away from the seated individual.

With eyes still closed, the seated individual is to guess who is standing by the chair using only his or her intuitive sensitivity to the other person's energy.

You'll be surprised how much fun this is and how quickly you'll be able to increase your sensitivity to spiritual energy.

In time, you'll also be able to easily feel the individual spiritual energy of your Angels around you even before they begin to communicate with you.

How do I really know I'm communicating with my Angels? How can I tell the difference between the information that comes from inside of me and the intuitive information I receive from my Angels?

As you speak with your Angels, you will undoubtedly feel and know that you are speaking with someone other than yourself.

How will you know this? Because your Angels will respond to your questions with answers that reflect their own unique and individual personalities.

Speaking with your Angels is very much like talking to a friend on the telephone. You call your friend, he/she answers the telephone, and you chat. Because you can't see him/her, you don't start doubting your friend's presence on the other line, wondering if perhaps you are just talking to yourself. That would seem ridiculous, wouldn't it? The more you practice, the greater your confidence that the intuitive information you are receiving is truly coming from your Angels.

If after practicing, however, you are still having difficulty differentiating between the information that is coming from your head and the information that is coming from your Angels, simply ask them to formally announce their presence before they begin speaking to you. Your Angels will make their presence known to you in a ''louder'' and less subtle form and you'll quickly be able to recognize them.

How can I help spiritually mentor my child?

Teach your children to have spiritual beliefs that include awareness of God and their guardian Angels. Discuss how Angels are assigned to them and why your children should continue to develop the natural relationship with their Angels that already exists.

It is very important for you to let your children know that you are open to discussing spiritual topics with them. If you laugh, dismiss, ignore, or argue with them about what they are sharing with you, they'll feel you are not interested or accepting and will probably not share any further information with you about their future encounters with their Angels. In addition, if they can't come to you as trusted parent with questions and concerns, who can they approach? You'll want to be the one who inspires and encourages your children to develop their spirituality.

Children learn by example. If you build your ability to channel with your Angels, your children will most likely be interested in following in your footsteps. Once you are successful in developing your channeling, it will be a very easy process for you to help your children build their ability to communicate with their Angels.

Ask to be introduced to your children's Angels. Then teach your children about their individual guardian Angels and introduce them by name. Explain to your children that their guardian Angels are best friends who will always have something special to talk about with them.

Children are truly unique, trusting little beings who

embody the honesty, unconditional love, and non-judgmental philosophy of life that is the pure essence of the Angelic spirit.

Angels have a special relationship with children because unlike adults, children are totally trusting and accepting of what their feelings and intuitive perceptions tell them about what they are experiencing.

This level of acceptance allows children to more effortlessly develop a relationship with their Angels because they do not rationalize or dismiss what they experience emotionally and spiritually.

If an Angel appears in a tangible form to a child, the child accepts the existence of the Angel just as he or she would accept the existence of another human being.

Angels have a much easier time communicating with children because a child will respond to channeling by attentively listening and trusting in what they see, feel, and hear without discrediting the encounter. When children casually mention an imaginary playmate, what they are often describing is the relationship they share with their guardian Angels.

In addition to ongoing encounters with their Angels, children are also frequently visited by other heavenly beings including deceased family members and soon-to-be-born siblings!

I was delighted when I received a telephone call from a client in New Jersey who just found out she was pregnant. She and her husband already had a three-year-old boy and she called to ask my opinion, as a friend, as to whether it was wise at that time to share the news about the pregnancy with her young son.

Following our discussion, she and her husband decided to wait a little while before they told the child.

Several months later the client called again to give me all the latest news about her family. Before she did so, she pointedly asked if I would channel to ask her Angels if her pregnancy would result in a girl or a boy.

When I asked for the information, I physically "saw" a little girl of about three who said that she wanted to give me the answer to my client's question.

The little girl told me that she was the child who was going to be coming into their family and that she had already been speaking with their young son, who was to be her future brother, to inform him of her arrival and to begin their brother-sister interaction.

My client gasped and replied, "I can't believe it!" She then proceeded to tell me about her little boy.

Until the previous day, she and her husband had still not shared the news of the pregnancy with their young son, and they believed he remained completely unaware that they were expecting a new arrival.

That morning at breakfast, the little boy casually mentioned that over the past several weeks, his "little sister" had spoken with him numerous times in his bedroom and that she "couldn't wait" to come and live with them. The little girl had given her brother the date of her arrival, which was almost identical to the due date the doctor had given my client.

The little boy went on to say that his "little sister" told him that she would be coming regularly to see him at night to talk so they could get acquainted and play together.

My client and her husband were astonished at what their young son had shared with them, but they did not dismiss or ignore his spiritual encounter. Instead they expressed openness and enthusiasm about his experience and asked him to repeat conversations with his sister any time they occurred in the future.

These nightly encounters persisted between the little boy and his sister until my client gave birth later that year to a beautiful, healthy baby girl who was eagerly awaited by her big brother.

Can channeling be used for bad or inappropriate purposes?

Just like any other skill or ability, channeling can be used for purposes other than for "the highest good."

As discussed in Chapter Nine, there are those psychics, palm readers, tarot card specialists, and other people in the metaphysical community who wish to develop and fine-tune their channeling ability to fraudulently "earn" money from unsuspecting clients. You must take care to ask for channeled information only from those you trust, or from those who come highly recommended. Trust your own instincts about the credibility, skill, and intentions of others who channel for you.

In addition, some people wish to develop their channeling ability to win money by gambling or from a lottery or similar contest.

It is important to remember that channeling with your guardian Angels or other heavenly beings is solely meant to help you work through issues, develop your enlightenment, and create a better quality of life for you and those around you.

If you misuse your ability, you won't lose it, but you'll be dramatically slowing down your progress in achieving personal, professional, and financial goals by foolishly focusing and investing your energy into something that is not meant to happen for your best benefit. You'll be creating a great deal more frustration, unhappiness, and dissatisfaction in your life if you force yourself to wait much longer for the realization of your dreams because of your pursuit of nonsensical or unethical financial goals.

If you are not meant to win the lottery or make a killing in Las Vegas, you'll never create the opportunity to do so, no matter how good a channel you become, unless winning the monies is directly related to helping you move forward spiritually.

Do I have to meditate to be a good channel?

Absolutely not! Meditation can provide a release from stress and pressure, and can help some individuals focus and regain their emotional and spiritual balance.

Meditation is not necessary, however, as a prerequisite to developing your ability to channel, nor to strengthen or maintain your inborn intuitiveness.

I recommend that you consider meditating as yet another form of recharging your batteries, much the same way as you would going to the movies, taking a walk in the park, eating foods you love, or going dancing.

How can I find out the names of my Angels and why they have been assigned to work with me?

After you have become "hooked in" and have developed a two-way communication with your Angels, simply ask them! They will be very eager to introduce themselves and explain exactly why they are working with you and what they hope to help you accomplish.

Are there any difficulties to avoid when you channel for someone else?

When I first started to channel for other people, I had no earthly idea what I would encounter.

From the start, I knew that I didn't need to worry about proteeting myself from weird or mischievous spirits because I was told by my Angels that such entities are not allowed to communicate or pass along any information during the channeling process.

What my Angels didn't tell me was that I needed to protect myself from the physical energy of my clients during the process of channeling!

If I did channeled reading for a client who had abdominal pain, I began to feel their abdominal pain. If I channeled for someone with nausea, I began to feel their nausea. It wasn't until I channeled for someone who had a terrible migraine headache that it began to occur to me that I quickly needed to do something to distance myself from absorbing my clients' physical energy.

I learned very quickly to put an invisible shield between myself and my client to avoid intuitively absorbing their physical maladies. I strongly recommend that you do the same.

In other words, before you start to channel, envision an armor-plated shield or cocoon of white light between you and the person for whom you're going to channel. In addition, ask your Angels to protect you from absorbing any of the other person's physical energy and you'll have no problems at all.

I often see my cat staring intently into thin air and meowing. Can animals see Angels?

Have you ever wondered why your pet stares with deep concentration at what appears to be a blank wall? Or why he/she seems to get suddenly excited when looking into thin air?

Like children, animals are fully sensitive to the existence of Angels and other heavenly beings. Your pets can see and hear your guardian Angels as well as your deceased loved ones. Your dog or cat will visibly react to a heavenly being and become immediately aware of their presence, sometimes long before we humans do! The next time your pet is reacting to an unseen presence, you may assume that you have one or several spiritual visitors.

Remember, you are being visited for a reason. Use the opportunity that Fluffy has made you aware of and work on your channeling!

✧❅❦❅✧

A Last Word

In each lifetime you are faced with an exciting journey that takes you on an unknown spiritual path that is very unique and individual. No one else has your talents and abilities, your issues to resolve, your past life history, or your particular life's purpose. How you decide to travel your spiritual path is completely up to you. Your quality of life is determined by how successfully you develop awareness, wisdom, and enlightenment while on your journey.

But every spiritual journey is clogged with impassable roadblocks, frustrating detours, and unexpected side trips that can slow our progress and even halt our forward movement altogether. There are times when we may find ourselves totally confused, empty, and depressed, as if we were emotionally and spiritually stranded by the side of the road, uncertain about who we are and where we are headed.

And just when you believe that you've totally lost your way, a soft voice urges you forward to continue your journey, providing a spiritual compass to bring you back to the awareness of where you are going, how long it will take to get there, and exactly what you'll encounter once you reach your destination.

The voices you hear are your Angels, and the wonderful, life-changing communication you can develop with them is called channeling.

If you listen, the voices of your Angels will be clear and unmistakable, offering support and encouragement to help you travel your spiritual path as happily and peacefully as possible. With the assistance of your Angels, you'll maintain the courage to continue on your journey and accomplish great things knowing that you will never travel alone. Your Angelic companions will nurture, sustain, guide, and protect you every step of the journey called life.